REFLECTIONS THROUGH
A JAUNDICED EYE

REFLECTIONS THROUGH A JAUNDICED EYE

ANDREW'S STORY

James McCurrach

authorHOUSE®

AuthorHouse™ LLC
1663 Liberty Drive
Bloomington, IN 47403
www.authorhouse.com
Phone: 1-800-839-8640

Published by AuthorHouse   01/09/2014

ISBN: 978-1-4918-2931-8 (sc)
ISBN: 978-1-4918-2932-5 (e)

Library of Congress Control Number: 2013919424

Any people depicted in stock imagery provided by Thinkstock are models, and such images are being used for illustrative purposes only. Certain stock imagery © Thinkstock.

This book is printed on acid-free paper.

Foreword

Andrew was a strange fellow. He had many good graces. He was brought up properly within a socially adept family. His brother and sister were much more outgoing and he often reflected on that fact. Towards the end of his life, he rather thought that he had it all figured out. Nice, but it didn't erase all the bad and there was plenty of that. He had no intention of being sorry for himself. There was no point in that and, besides, his mom had always stuck by him while emphasizing that one needed to "keep up the spirits" and "play the hand" that was given to him. Optimism had been deeply ingrained and a very, very good thing that it was. He could easily have given up at many points along the way. He didn't and wouldn't. On the other hand, he was no Pollyanna—never believed that one could afford to sit back and adopt an attitude of "everything will turn out for the best" Ugh! Just hearing it (or writing it now) upset him. For better or worse, he always kept moving forward—often in the wrong direction. Yet, he always resurrected himself despite the conflicts and his own wrongheadedness. He generally avoided pointing "fingers" but as he aged, certain traits and habits became much clearer. And the facts tended to support his actions. He knew, for instance, that sex had consumed him for the first sixty years of his life—consumed him to the extant of driving all of his actions. Early on as a bank employee he wanted to travel as it would give him an entrée into different cities and different sexual outlets. And he worked as a teacher in good part because it kept him close to youthful males. It seemed to be never ending and, yet, it was in direct conflict with his sense of family and the need to settle down. He had trampled over several relationships that led to suicides and, still, he wouldn't stop. Serial sexual activity became the norm and would not cease until advancing age interrupted his sexual drive. He was just lucky in finally having a partner who was forgiving and would stand by him. Without that he could easily have been left alone to sulk in solitary abandonment. It was an ego thing, no doubt about that—a bad inner image that took years to set aside. He couldn't escape blame for his actions but certainly being the first born son brought up in his father's image was a distinct disadvantage. His dad would never let up, never give any encouragement, never hugged him and complimented him on a job "well done". As a result, Andrew never felt very comfortable in his own skin and found himself always trying to outdo dad while at the same time wanting to "punish" dad for mistreating him. It was a bad formula for success and, indeed, success would be elusive until late in life when he would finally become his own person. Into this difficult "mix" would be added the homosexuality which more than "muddied" the water—especially at a time when it was a condition that "dare not speak its name". As Andrew entered into his 70th year and was more settled down, he found himself reflecting more and more—reliving the past and trying to make some sense of it all. Bringing it into the open. Churning the specifics would help—even if his eyes were slightly jaundiced.

REFLECTIONS THROUGH A JAUNDICED EYE

ANDREW'S STORY

REFLECTIONS ETC. ETC.

ANDREW RARELY NEEDED AN ALARM clock to get him going—at any rate not since the arrival of his so-called Golden Years. This wasn't surprising in light of the fact that he had constructed his life with a great sense of discipline. He even managed to discipline his drinking. When he thought back on it (which was often) life took on an incessant regularity. There always seemed to be a time and place for everything. He thought this was just grand at the time it took place but, as life moved on, he wondered if he wasn't a borderline case of insanity. He more or less rationalized that by telling himself that work for him had kept him functioning on what most would consider an acceptable level. Still, there were moments that bordered on the criminal and even a few times when what he did was specifically against the law. Still, he was basically a good citizen and criminology generally came into play only out of necessity when facing a bottomed out checkbook. The years had had passed by in a blur. No big surprise in that although now he was getting closer to the end. He couldn't imagine life without life and looked upon his state of being as a forever condition. He did, however, admit to others and any who cared to listen that the end could come at any moment. He didn't allow it to interfere with daily routines although he now had little room for trivia. This occasionally bordered on antisocial behavior but Andrew found that he got much more done that way. This was in direct contrast to his lover who might loosely be described as a "social animal". It would often lead to disagreements and sometimes anger but even that had mellowed with the passage of time. At this late stage, he and his lover had been together for more than thirty years.

On this particular chilly December morning, Andrew's inner clock followed its usual pattern of turning him over and informing him that it was time to get moving. His mind did its usual flip-flop and that too was part of the routine. Further, the routine also included what he intended to accomplish on that particular day. He always mentally detailed it quite specifically, and, usually completed what he set out to do. And even at his tender age (79) there was still time for five minutes devoted to fantasy images of younger people (boys) who might have crossed his path in the last 24 hours. Andrew was not a pedophile in the strict sense of the word. He would never force himself on a youngster. He knew all too well that it could mess them up psychologically and, besides, he abhorred taking advantage no matter what the age. He also couldn't imagine going to jail and, so, his thoughts were a nice fantasy outlet but nothing more. Dream objects had long been available as Andrew had been a teacher for quite some time. This brought him into daily contact with the young and beautiful. It helped his moods and kept him on an even keel. The visuals also helped him get to sleep and were particularly comforting stuff as old-age established itself. Sometimes he thought back to former mutual consenting connections. Today, Andrew's mind was unusually active and contemplative. He gave thanks for the calming effect of his dream world but the reality of the upcoming day's activities was much more important. At the same time, he found himself retreating—reaching way back looking for explanations. It was probably a little premature to sum up all that had transpired over the years. On that score, he sometimes grasped at the air and didn't understand the how or why. He did take comfort in believing that he was a good person. That didn't really do much to define him and it needed much more fine tuning. There were still lots of unanswered questions—questions with answers that needed to be brought together. He had been trying to do just that for years although often deep thoughts had eluded him.

Routine!—It's part of all of us or should be as most of us have to go to work to support ourselves thus making routine a part of the work ethic. Sometimes, routines exceeded common sense. His brother would remain in a job that he didn't enjoy yet stuck with it for forty years. He never realized that life was short and opportunities decreased as age advanced. Of course, work was only a small part of the overall equation. Besides, the world had changed and job security was more ephemeral. Andrew remembered his dad always talking about job security. His dad had been one of those so-called business" freaks" who thought that the sun would never set on major United States corporations. His dad's most prominent example was General Motors which for dad could do no wrong. And the company carried on for quite some time until some of the post-World War II countries caught up and temporarily put General Motors out of business. In a smirking sort of way, it made Andrew chuckle. He had never much agreed with his dad as he tended to be very selective when it came to setting examples. At any rate, the world had changed and the big corporate security blanket was no more. General Motors was just one of the many who would be forced to downsize in order to survive. So much for job security! In some cases the loss of a job was only one of many problems. Even pensions and health benefits were disappearing. The orderly world was also changing and was upsetting the equilibrium on all sides. Working attitudes also took on a different dimension. People now were more attuned to maximizing returns and if that meant change, then change it would be. The Internet only increased the flexibility. Andrew appreciated the new attitudes and rather liked the way it affected his surroundings. It made people infinitely more aware and more interesting while broadening their experiences.

Reflections!—It had been an unusually reflective morning. Maybe it had something to do with the weather. His mother always referred to gray skies as "yucky" and "yucky" it was today. Andrew had adapted many of his mother's phases and they had stayed with him over the years. Mom always played a major part in his reflective aura. She was never far away except when he was locked into his sexual fantasy world. And it just so happened that this morning he had actually woken up in a horny state of mind. That didn't happen quite as frequently now. After crossing the 65-year-old age level he noticed that erections were less frequent. They sometimes still happened on command but more and more they needed visual stimuli. (Internet videos). He had also more and more come to rely on one of those small blue pills that had been the salvation of many problematic relationships. Without that pill, he rather thought that his sex life might have disappeared—something that would be borderline disaster in light of living with a partner who was 15 years his junior.

Generally, the state of horniness was often part of the wake-up call (even without an erection). In more productive times, mornings had been the locus of some of his most pleasurable orgasms. He supposed that that had a great deal to do with the fact that a night of rest and recharging his batteries had heightened his nerve endings. For as long as he could remember, mornings always arrived with a great deal of energy. His partner, Josh, always teased him about his so-called whirling dervish effect. It didn't bother Andrew; indeed be appreciated the high energy level. He just wished that it came with more frequent erections. He couldn't do much about that and his doctor told him that it was quite common in older gentleman. That sounded a little bit ominous to Andrew but he let it pass and just hoped that it didn't signal clogged arteries or some other serious malady. Lord knows, his father had problems of his own which were all too often inherited. Then again, dad had never given much thought to taking care of himself and had wallowed in regular breakfasts of bacon and eggs and a dinner centered around red meat. Andrew was sure that it had also affected his father's sex life although any sex discussion was always off limits.

At least his day and gotten off to a good start with that welcome erection. Best of all, it had stayed that way rather than softening as his mind wandered to what he hoped he would accomplish during the next twenty four hours. It was as if his highly valued cock was calling for some attention. But—what to do with it? Josh lay next to him but Andrew (he hated to be called Andy) was afraid to initiate any action without that little blue pill. He had occasionally tried to take unmedicated action but it had resulted in unsatisfactory results. This had psyched him out and he didn't want to try again. He had never been particularly successful in turning to other sources of inspiration such as pictures of young boys, or, naked beauties on the Internet. Internet bodies were the stuff of dreamworld thrills but were far removed from reality. All of this brought back another wispy moment from Andrew's memory bank—a time when Andrew actually went so far as to hire one of those escort boys. One could have the pick of the litter by ordering up according to hair color, body shape, and type of action desired.It seemed like a great idea on the surface but as it played out, Andrew would lose interest knowing that the boy couldn't have cared less and only wanted to get paid. At least he learned something about himself in that you needed a bed mate with genuine feelings. Sex for hire was still out there with thousands of beauties available for viewing (and more). There were so many images—where did they come from and how did they pass the hours in a regular eight hour working day?

Back in the real world Andrew's mind drifted elsewhere and the erection subsided. Sometimes he thought it would be nice to spend an entire day in dreamland. Yet, he was too much of a realist and, in fact, he reflected back way too much. There always seemed to be a steady stream of triggers that brought back the past. Still, the immediate always took precedence as Andrew always wanted to keep moving forward. Now, he conjured up his to do list as he was at heart a "doer" and a compulsive one at that. He hated loose ends. His partner had a different take on that. He and Josh were clear-cut examples of opposites attracting one another. For Josh, loose ends were everywhere and procrastination ruled the day. It bothered Andrew a lot and for a time he thought he might even leave the nest. Instead, he had developed a system whereby he shut out Josh's bad habits. Josh needed to change but if he was going to do that it had to come from within and would never happen at Andrews direction.

Sex might have been set aside that morning (and other mornings as well) but sex continued to dominate a vast amount of his daily thinking. Indeed, he had become obsessed with it even before entering his teenage years. He made numerous attempts to push it into the background but it never worked. He never did understand the why of it all and eventually gave up wondering and could do little more than try and control himself. It wasn't easy! Every day seemed to be filled at least partially with one sexual image or another. At least he was disciplined enough not to let it overwhelm him although visuals were always lurking.

Enough daydreaming! It was time to get on with the day's activity. He couldn't do anything about the "yucky" weather but plans were afoot today outside of his normal activities. Too bad that the day had gotten off to a poor start as his partner had had another one of those nasty meltdowns. These always involved angry exchanges that made Andrew cringe and want to run away. Instead, he never argued back referring instead to bury within himself. Over the course of the years he had done a good job freezing out the anger. It had not been easy and, worse, it had established a barrier to total honesty between the two of them. It also made for continuing discomfort. Andrew tried to rationalize all of this by emphasizing the good side of their relationship. Allot of the good had centered around their sexual compatibility but age had taken a toll on that, bringing the many personality differences into focus. On this particular morning in question, Josh was complaining about the cold temperature within the house. Complaints tended to escalate and this morning had been more of the same. It put an end to all sexual hopes. More reflections interfered as Andrew dreamed of what might have been. He was trapped and knew it and good or bad he was going to make the best of it. He wished Josh would stop worrying so much and go with the flow better. Of course, he had to share the blame and he was always ready to do that. Josh, unfortunately, never accepted the fact that he might be at fault. He was always finger-pointing and sending blame in another direction. Andrew never could understand that particular personality trait or where it had originated (inferiority complex?). Anyway, it was a little too late to do anything about it. Andrew just had to accept the incompleteness of their relationship. Andrew was such an idealist and that wasn't entirely a good thing. He expected too much and disappointments always happened. Additionally, he had always wanted to stay in control and that was surely not a healthy attribute. He tried to exhibit the control gently but that need for domination was always there and had created additional imbalances.

Enough with the introspection! it had gone on too long now and was taxing his aging brain. It also depressed him, made him wish that he was better, made him wish that he could be more understanding and more of an equal partner. Instead, there was lopsidedness whereby he always had to act the boss. He was fortunate in being a loyal soul and, combined with native intelligence, had kept the partnership together. He surely didn't want to spend his last days alone and, so, compromise became the necessary ingredient. He also did not like surprises and worked even harder at keeping the peace. This took some effort as surprises were more or less part of the daily diet—always present in one form or another. Josh thought Andrew was obsessed and he was to a certain extent. They were something of a a crazy couple—Andrew always wanting to keep the peace and Josh often a nervous worrier. At least they managed to share a great deal together. There were all of those wonderful orgasms but there were also common enjoyments—the theater, movies, museums, anything that involved art of one sort or another. Sometimes it was hard for Andrew to accentuate the positive and with aging limitations intruding, this task had become even more difficult. And with less sex, Josh's temper seemed to flare even more. This only made the sexual act even more remote and made Andrew appreciate even more the Internet images. On the other hand, he was smart enough to know that a seventy nine year-old man would have little in common with a 22 year old internet boy. The beauty was one thing but living together was an entirely different matter. Josh didn't quite understand that, resenting the fact that Andrew sometimes turned to younger images.

It was now time to head out to work. Morning work now consisted of part-time librarian duties with the afternoons devoted to teaching. Library work was pretty straightforward while teaching was always a complicated mix. There were always the good students who wanted to learn but there were also the misfits who could make it very nerve-wracking. Sometimes, the bad boys would decide to grow up but that usually didn't happen until years after graduation. Andrew had tried to take it all with a grain of salt having long since realized that every occupation came with its bad side. Teaching had once been a full-time career but in the midst of discipline problems, Andrew had decided to back off and limit his work to part-time duty. He had at least exited on a positive note. And for the last couple of years the students seemed to be more motivated and with fewer bad habits. Quite a change over the earlier years when the headmaster had largely opened the admission doors to support a wife with expensive habits. Soon there were too many students with substance abuse problems and classrooms harder to control. Andrew's idealistic bubble had been burst and had brought into question the viability of his full-time staying power. The headmaster had wrongly put the onus on Andrew for his lack of control. Andrew tried very hard to keep the peace and had stayed with the school despite the problem cases which had multiplied from two or three to over a dozen. Through it all he had enjoyed being around youth. He knew there was a sexual "angle" to it even though his intentions were always honorable. Indeed, he took care to avoid any discussion of a sexual subject matter having learned his lesson early on when he had made an offhand remark about circle jerking. That expression managed to float around the school for weeks making Andrew determined to keep discussions 100% clean. He did still imagine what many of them would look like in a state of undress since he couldn't help but appreciate youthful beauty. As Andrew was something of a hairy beast, he particularly admired the young Asian boys with their hairless bodies and smooth skin. He liked being surrounded by the boys and liked to think it helped give him a positive outlook. This, in turn, helped keep him in good mental shape. Of course, he had also obsessively exercised and that that certainly played a big part in keeping his body physically fit.

It had been the headmaster who had politely suggested that Andrew consider part-time employment. Gently put perhaps, but Andrew knew it was take it or leave it. At least it would keep him in the mix at school even though teaching would now be a small part of his overall responsibilities. He would still have a classroom but now he would be working solely with foreign students having limited capabilities with the English language. This did give him the potential for small rewards as the kids progressed in mastering English. However, any complex knowledge of world history was stymied by the lack of understanding intricacies. Still, Andrew swallowed his pride and tried to make the best of his limited options. He also rationalized that he was probably lucky to still be there in the first place. A bad economy had taken its toll on private school enrollment. From a high of 110 students, the school had now been reduced to 65. At least the quality was better but the viability of the school was in question. Staff cuts had been made and the Headmaster had been released and replaced by the headmaster's oldest daughter. In addition to his negligible classroom responsibilities, Andrew's teaching schedule would also include responsibility for the school's athletic endeavors. That was something of a joke in light of the limited enrollment. It sounded impressive but the task, in truth, wasn't much of anything. The largest parcel of work consisted of policing 60% of the students who turned to outside sources for exercise. This meant that they took it upon themselves to go to gyms, dance studios, or karate or yoga classes. Andrew was responsible for making sure that these students were actually following through on their exercise commitments. Not a lot of brainpower involved and, indeed, he regarded it as" pain in the ass" duty. Additionally, he would also be responsible for in-house exercise. This consisted of twice a week basketball at a neighboring court and twice a week soccer in Golden gate Park. Nice! except that the reality was something else. Limited students meant limited action and the headmaster didn't help by introducing too many after school activities which interfered with the sports program. Andrew had tried to find more rewarding work elsewhere but his age had long mitigated against that. Combined with the bad economy he was essentially locked in and unable to move on. Money was, of course, much less than what he had earned as a full-time employee but at least it would help keep them afloat each month

Andrew sometimes reflected back and wondered what his father might have thought of his predicament. Of course, dad would never have found himself there in the first place. Teaching almost certainly would have been at the bottom of his dad's wish list. No doubt his wanting to teach bore some direct relation to removing himself from the stigma of his dad's lifestyle. Part of a conscious master plan serving as retribution for the sins Andrew had suffered in childhood. And Andrew never wanted to go back, never wanted to revisit the past. He never could understand how his partner could spend so much time viewing old Hollywood films that he had already seen several times over. For Andrew there was so much that was new and, besides, most of the past was ugly. At least he could take comfort in knowing that he had broken loose and become his own person. It had taken him some time to remove himself from those old influences and, indeed, he still retained some of his dad's habits (bad) and personality quirks (unattractive). It had left him with a sad hangover and had a way of showing up from time to time when Josh would tell him that he still had a lot of his dad inside him. He also was still largely stuck in his ways (Josh's expression) but at least he was at long last the ruler of his own "kingdom"—something that had never existed while his dad was still alive. Unfortunately, he also lacked any motivation to get ahead—at least in the business sense of the word. A bad combination when partnered with a wealthy upbringing and his appreciation for the good things in life. In one sense, he envied his brother and sister whose wealth would keep them in comfort until their dying days. Not so with Andrew who had generally made a mess of his vocations. Even the teaching fulfillment had come too late and then had managed in large part to disintegrate around him.

No matter the age, he liked to think that it was never too late to move on, even if he had no intention of upsetting the general order of things. In truth, Josh would always be there and Andrew couldn't really imagine himself outside of the deep-seated relationship that had developed over the course of many years. Andrew had accepted the fact that all relationships have their good and bad sides. What he didn't appreciate was the fact that the last year had seen the predominance of the bad. Stress had arrived with a capital "S" as Josh had problems with his mother and a wayward brother. Josh had never been very good at dealing with stress. He had grown up with the proverbial "silver spoon" and, like Andrew, his good native intelligence had given him an appreciation for the finer things in life. And there were other similarities. Like Andrew, Josh had never had much ambition and expected the man to carry the financial burden(Andrew being the man). Obviously, this hadn't worked and the money cracks that eventually appeared would only accentuate the stress. Josh was just plain too sensitive about everything or, as he put it, he felt everything deeply. This was great when frolicking in bed but quite another matter when day-to-day responsibilities demanded attention. The nerve ends would break and the anger would surface. At times it seemed as if there was no organization and that a comfortable structure was nonexistent. Andrew worked hard at avoiding surprises but surprises were inevitable.

In sum, Andrew kept struggling along the same old path at school. The change to a part time status was largely anticlimactic. And working at the library had kept him surrounded in large part by youth, particularly one employee(Kyle) who was very sensual with a lovely body and bedroom eyes. Sadly, there were few new challenges at the library and little opportunity to contribute in a meaningful way. Librarians were a special breed and Andrew wondered whatever motivated one to become a librarian. Maybe it all started at an early age, much like one wanting to be a fireman or policeman. It did involve a commitment as one had to get a degree in Library Science (whatever that was). Librarians seemed like a nice bunch and Andrew had gotten to know quite a few of them. Kyle was certainly the main attraction, motivating Andrew to apply for the job in the first place. Andrew hadn't quite figured him out but that was okay. He just liked being around him and often imagined him naked which served to inspire numerous erections.

Andrew's reading habits brought forth more reflections. He was thinking too much although appreciated his own curious nature which was at the heart of his heavy reading habit. He took to reading with a vengeance at the conclusion of his college years. He had initially been attracted to novels—popular ones that had showed up on bestseller lists. Maybe it had something to do with his need to feel trendy! It had been a costly exercise in that Andrew was purchasing rather than borrowing. Eventually, he would hold a book sale while at the same time switching his reading allegiance to works of non fiction. Most of this centered around biographies where he found lots of fascinating stories. Friends admired his reading determination and the whole process kept his brain active while further stimulating his curious nature. There was a downside to all this reading and that was that it kept him within himself. This eventually meant additional conflicts with Josh who regarded the reading as largely a mechanism for escape.(true to a certain extent). Of course, for Andrew it helped simplify matters while helping to avoid controversy. Over the years, avoiding controversy became significantly more important. In this sense, Andrew's private world became more and more the center of his universe although he regarded that with mixed emotions. Reading might have satisfied his learning needs but it was also symptomatic of a further retreat from life. Josh had a much different take on that and almost seemed purposefully to go in the opposite direction. This made for more conflicts and, for Andrew, his private world became more and more the center of his universe. Also, Andrew didn't mix well with Josh's circle of young friends. Those friends were largely a makeshift bunch with all kinds of anxieties and emotional disturbances. Josh was awfully good at providing a warm shoulder and good advice which was far removed from Andrew's own capabilities. It was not surprising that Andrew had few friends while Josh had almost too many. Andrew knew that his lack of friends was a defect and could be traced back to his teenage years when friendships were harder to come by. Now there was much more openness along with Internet sources. It was almost too complicating nowadays and sometimes Andrew yearned for the simplicity of his youth. He worked hard at maintaining certain simplicities-always trying to bring routines down to the lowest common denominator. There were those same timely wake-up calls, the same breakfast habits and, generally, the same workaday habits . . . It made for sleep filled nights—quite different from his dad who hated the night and took all manner of potions to fall asleep. That made no sense to Andrew as his dad had few worries and had retired with a comfortable "nest egg". Back in those days there was also little indebtedness so for many there were few financial worries. There were no credit cards and loans were agreed upon by simple handshakes. It simplified communication although like most everything else, there was a downside to it all. Children were brought up in blissful ignorance of a great deal—particularly anything unpleasant. As a grown-up, Andrew disagreed with that while still reaching out for simplicity. Routines made it all seem easy. Even his schoolwork followed a set pattern. And the nighttime hours were simplified as well. Depending on the season, there were only a few television shows that he followed. Then again, there were few options. Now,though, channel availability had grown exponentially. (Did people really need 250 channels of entertainment and TV movie options in the hundreds?). Present-day children just had too many diversions. Young minds were now bombarded by video games, cell phones, to say nothing of other Internet distractions. It's a wonder that kids made any sense at all. In the face of all this Andrew stayed with the simple life. Even his playtime had become routine—a Saturday night out for dinner (preceded by a rum cocktail at home). Occasionally he diverted but only if Josh insisted. Fortunately for Andrew, there weren't many of those situations. There were movies, of course, and the occasional theater "piece" but these were largely programmed to fit into certain time frames. Variations were rare and Andrew didn't much like it when schedules were altered.

All this need for a strict routine had started when Andrew was in college. Almost overnight he had matured and set himself on a very strict course. Earlier, immaturity had followed him at every turn. He blamed his father for his internal revolts, reaching out to fight back from fatherly demands. At least he had finally turned things around and woken up to the fact that it made much more sense to keep the peace and do something positive with his life. He had also gotten tired of causing trouble and being on the wrong side of his father's moods. So it was that college became a success. He was convinced that a good portion of that success came about through his policy of set routines. Internal disciplines were established and extended everywhere. He rather liked the way it all turned out. It even made his two-year Army stint a comfortable occurrence. It had been something of a struggle at first but eventually he easily cohabited with the Army's rules of law.

Time for work! And off to the library. He was always dutiful about his every work schedule. He was always on time and always present and accounted for; indeed, over his long life and several jobs he could boast of a perfect attendance record. A notable achievement although not done for any reason of grandstanding. Rather, it was part of his nature, one of the few good things his dad had passed on to him. Dad had lived through the catastrophe of the Depression and it gave him the respect for any and all jobs, no matter how menial. He looked forward to the library. It seemed like a perfect fit as he could do it in conjunction with his afternoon school responsibilities. It also kept him close to his beloved reading habits and, hopefully, even closer to beautiful Kyle. Indeed, after first meeting Kyle he had made inquiries about library work. It surprised him a little bit that they would "cotton" to someone his age (he still didn't think much about age) but the library turned out to place more emphasis on wisdom, something that they said often came with age. Upon further inquiry, he learned that there was little salary differential from part-time teaching. Actually, that wasn't particularly surprising since nobody became a teacher for its salary perks. People often chided him about all the extra vacation time but he regarded that with the proverbial "grain of salt". Good teaching was always hard work so that any time off was well earned. Library work, at least, was largely hassle free and had that added benefit of working in a highly literate atmosphere.

As in most low-paying jobs, library workers came and went. This was understandable as most of the staff were young and only working there while completing on various educational requirements. Still, a good percentage of employees had a relatively lengthy time in grade—no doubt at least partially a reflection of the positive attitude that prevailed. The easy give-and-take attitude was especially prevalent with the more sophisticated and better educated librarians. They could converse constructively on many levels and there was something quite heartening about it all.

Obviously, it was too late for Andrew to take up the study of library science but he certainly had enough intelligence to make a difference with those who trafficked through the library. He only hoped that he would have enough patience to work it properly. Discipline was important but that was generally true anywhere. Besides, Andrew was a pretty good disciplinarian and enjoyed being busy. He had tried to fill every waking hour with some sort of busyness. He just hoped that he was mellow enough to tolerate the relatively non-challenging nature of the library job. He was sure he could do it. The only problem that he could foresee was where in the system he would land. The library had many branches outside of its principal downtown location. He had been to many of the branches outside of the one closest to school. He feared that he might be assigned to a poorer neighborhood or even the main building downtown. That headquarters building had a bad reputation for loitering as well as some unruly, homeless people who looked upon it as a temporary refuge. There were rules against all this but being selective about who came in and out was close to impossible. Library staffers tended to be low key people who always wanted to avoid a ruckus. Andrew had witnessed an occasional scene but there weren't many of them. He just hoped that he could avoid an assignment in a poorer neighborhood.

He lucked out, but in the long run it would only be a partial victory. In a matter of weeks, he had been called in for an interview with some stuffy senior employment administrator who looked like everybody's image of the perfect librarian. They had obviously been in the system for quite some time. He got the usual rigamarole about being overqualified (no doubt about that) but there was some good give-and-take about Andrew's life experiences to date. It might best have been described as a good verbal "soapbox" (he loved sounding off when given the appropriate opening). Of course, he spent most of his time talking about his love of books and his long love affair with the library. He had won the day and it pleased him to learn that most of his time would be spent working at the branch where it all began (and where Kyle worked). It satisfied him to think that it was all meant to be.

He was glad to be heading out! As much as he liked his privacy, the thought of being partially homebound held no appeal at all. He needed to interact, even if there was a sexual motivation to it. He wasn't particularly proud of his sexual obsession but had come to accept it as being a primary motivating force. It was just a significant part of his makeup—even before he entered his teenage years. The visuals of interacting fueled his fantasies and that very much helped get him through the day. Better that than having to depend on the internet for inspiration. He still clung to sexual images racing through his head but age had made it more difficult to "awaken" his penis. No longer would it become an automatic event. Rather, it needed "new blood" to get it going. Kyle at the library could "trigger" the arousal "button"—he could feel the sensation in his groin whenever their paths crossed. In effect, that told him that further physical togetherness would surely make him very hard. The only problem with that was that it was unlikely to happen since Kyle and other young objects of desire were usually not willing partners to such activity. Then again, he could be wrong. God only knows how many opportunities were missed because he held back and wasn't more forthright about his desires.

Chapter **2**

SEX

THERE HAD NEVER BEEN ANY disputing Andrew's sex drive. It was always front and center and had sadly been his major motivating force. He could vividly recall his first orgasm which had actually felt a little weird to him. No doubt the location had something to do with it and had seriously contributed to a sense of confusion over what should have been a seminal moment. He was barely 12 years old and there was nothing particularly romantic about it. The only good thing that came out of it was that it set the stage for later negative feelings about anonymous sex. He had been in a school bathroom using the facilities when approached by an older student. Oddly enough, the boy turned out to be the captain of the football team. Andrew had offered no resistance since he had no idea of what was happening. The orgasm had stayed with him for quite some time as he tried to assimilate the significance of it all. It was surely a pleasant enough sensation despite giving off those feelings of guilt. The guilt, however, was trumped by a need for more. At the time, he wished that he could have talked to somebody about it but that had proven to be an impossible task. He sensed that what had transpired was not a normal occurrence and, as such, he had avoided relating the experience to his parents. That was all well and good since the whole subject of sex had never surfaced on the home front. His mom had occasionally made "off kilter" remarks about "pansies" and men who might be (as she put it) "light in their loafers". For Andrew, that had been more than enough to tell him that having sex with another male was out of bounds and beyond normality. Still, it quite intrigued Andrew and he even sought out his football sex partner thinking that they might repeat the experience, albeit under better circumstances. Despite not understanding what had transpired, perhaps the experience might have a more pleasurable outcome were the two of them fully naked and in a more comfortable setting. Somehow, reaching across a urinal as in their first meeting, seemed more like an act of desperation. Still, there was no denying the handsomeness of his bathroom mate and Andrew was in part flattered that such a handsome specimen would want to mingle with him. Right at that point in time Andrew was not much to look at. He was slightly pudgy and his so-called coke bottle glasses didn't add anything to his appeal. Maybe his bathroom escapade was nothing more than a case of being in the right place at the right time along with his appearing vulnerable (or, as they say: it takes one to know one). Andrew wondered what kind of radar he had displayed. Was something this important obvious to everybody? All of a sudden, so many questions. Unfortunately, try as he might there would be no further contact with the football star. They would make eye contact a couple of times but Andrew didn't like the message that was being relayed. It spelled rejection but at least Andrew could gloat after watching several football games. He knew all too well that underneath all that football clothing there was beauty to behold.

This newfound sex business was proving to be very frustrating. Should he emphasize the guilt or concentrate on the joys? The boys were certainly much more appealing than the girls and the boys in his Elementary School were a particularly attractive group. The boys tended to be better bred and good breeding stock tended to produce clean cut looking children. Many years later Andrew could reconstruct some of those handsome faces and could even recall those names who had particularly struck his fancy. At the time, he really appreciated being amongst all this young beauty. It was nothing short of "mind-boggling" while also making him feel inadequate. He knew that he wasn't much to look at and that there wasn't much he could do about that at the time (he would take care of that later). Almost immediately he started to fantasize about what some of them might look like in a state of undress. He had to keep all this to himself for, as noted, sex was a taboo subject and way outside the limits of normal conversation. One time he inadvertently entered his parents bedroom without knocking (he was impatient about something) and found them in the midst of the sexual act. His dad had later carried on for days, angry at the "dastardly" intrusion. Aside from interrupting a heightened moment, Andrew got the distinct impression that children should not be exposed to such activity at an early age. For Andrew, it only reinforced feelings of guilt although it did nothing to interfere with his growing attraction for his male classmates.

It would be some time before a new physical opportunity presented itself. During that long stretch, Andrew found that his attraction to other males had only intensified. Indeed, he had actually commenced his own form of daily mind games. It would be his own inner hit parade covering his sixth-grade classmates. This list would change weekly but was always based on pure physical attraction. Since there was little opportunity for naked viewing, the list, out of necessity, depended on dress, athletic appearance or some specific form of communication. At the time, Andrew wasn't much of an athlete so there was little reason for him to prowl about locker rooms. Besides, he was much too shy to do such a thing. So, he continued to reside in his guessing world which, of course, had little basis in reality. Nevertheless, he quite enjoyed the daily visual exercise. There was something quite pleasurable in conjuring up all those images of beauty even though he suspected that pure nakedness might reveal something very different from what was circulating in his head. In its odd, perverse way, going to school every day meant a great deal more than pure learning.

The next set of climaxes were self induced and came with much more pleasure than guilt. Getting aroused had become the new normal. He could dictate erections almost at will merely by conjuring up any number of fantasy dreamscapes. He also found that he could heighten the feelings if he wrote about them while stroking himself. He conjured up all manner of perfect worlds where he was naked with one classmate or another. He was amazed at how excited it could get him and how difficult it was sometimes to hold back the orgasm. Where did all this come from? Was his homosexuality an attempt to be his father's opposite? He rather thought that it made little sense that his sex drive had been determined in the womb. Whatever, he wasn't complaining and rather enjoyed his status.

Masturbation was not, however, entirely rewarding. It had no lasting effect beyond a single moment of release. Still, he was young and it was easy enough to start all over. More than once he would return to his fantasy world two or three times a day—especially when school let out early. He worried a little bit about being insatiable so he made a concerted effort not to let it overtake his life. He had been facilitated in all of this by the privacy of his living quarters which were tucked away on the 3rd floor of the family residence. In their own way, his parents were contributing to his private sex life and he was far enough away so that he could hear anyone approaching in his direction. His sex life did tend to complicate his friendship attempts since physical attraction played such a dominant part. He had never been very good at making friends in the first place and now onrushing puberty had made him even more self-contained and more of a loner. He would gravitate to those having sexual appeal and that wasn't always a very good thing. It also upset him that the best looking boys had discussions that centered around girls. Still, one night in the midst of all this he had a serious conversation with himself and decided on a new tack. He would make a greater effort to seek out friendships. These might have sexual overtones but he would try to keep the sex possibilities in the background. He did, nevertheless, gravitate towards the more sensitive types as they better fed his ego. Much later, as he entered the 8th grade, he would gravitate to a tall, handsome blonde (almost an albino). Blondes were always at the top of his list (opposites attract—his own hair was a dark mop). Andrew thought that this particular boy was perfection personified. He was a "whitey" on all counts with smooth, creamy skin. (sixty years later he would remember every detail of their interaction). The boy had a nice personality as well. The end result was a series of mutual one on one togetherness session. These came, out of after school get together. Lots of running around in a very big yard would often be followed by rough housing that was general and exciting for Andrew. It was all not very rewarding but at least it was some private contact with another classmate. If nothing else, the visuals and touching were great even though what transpired was essentially a one-way street. He just hoped that he himself wasn't inadequate. Andrew wanted more but the boy hastily buttoned up and just as quickly was out the door and on his bicycle and heading home. Nary a word passed between them and so Andrew had no sense of his friend's feelings. It all wasn't much but at least it opened a small window in Andrew's limited sex world. He had read somewhere about sex addicts who were seemingly never satisfied. That sounded like a terrible curse—especially for Andrew who couldn't imagine being controlled by anything or anyone. Bad enough that dad was already so controlling. He wanted no more of that and realized that he might have to work at an increasingly high level to keep his sex drive within some sort a reasonable perspective. He was already spending an inordinate amount of time with his hit parade list. It was already a one-hour activity although he did eventually cut back. Still he could do little about his frequent states of arousal which occurred unexpectedly at a sporting event or from some unusual contacts in the classroom or hallways. Most assuredly the sex drive was only getting stronger and he needed an even greater effort to hold it back. As he started his teenage years, his brain would become even more compartmentalized. He needed to do that so that he could keep everything in order even though it drove him to further isolation. The ugly part of it all was that real friendships were more and more beyond him since his socializing always had a sexual subtext.

Puberty arrived when he was 13. It was not easy dealing with puberty and the resulting roaring sex drive. He sensed that most of his associates were having a much easier time of it. They may have been partially confused about sex longings but their attractions centered mostly on their female opposites. Andrew, of course, still hadn't figured it all out although there was no disputing the physical attraction he felt for other males. Frustrations had only grown stronger as had his search for additional male physical companionship. He now tried a new approach. Along with after school activities, some of the students would participate in sleepovers. This was largely a female occupation but some of the boys did it as well. Boy sleepovers tended to be very different from what went on with the girls. Boys talked more about sports and TV watching (TV was in its infancy but his dad had already purchased a set). There was some sneaky smoking but not much else. Over the course of several weeks, Andrew had conscientiously developed a plan of action. He would approach what he thought were good potential candidates, emphasizing those who had displayed some sense of sweetness and sensitivity.

Once again he would luck out! Roger would turn out to be compliant in that he was unsure of himself sexually. He was very handsome—slightly stocky but possessing lovely curly hair and a great smile. Many years later he would remember Roger all too well (he even liked the name). The enjoyment of sharing their bodies would stay with him for weeks. Again it was a masturbatory situation but at least they were naked on a bed and brought each other to climax. Andrew had enjoyed it so much that he struggled to hold himself back from premature ejaculation. He surely could have done much more (kissing, oral sex) but was fearful of taking it any further. That one time with Roger would be the extent of their physical contact and they would end up being little more than nodding acquaintances. For a time Roger leaped to the top of the hit parade list. Unfortunately, after Roger there would be a long dry spell. It would be summer and school was out and the lovely visuals were no longer concentrated in one place. Andrew had heard some rumors about other students having homosexual proclivities but those usually exhibited female characteristics and held no appeal for Andrew. There was actually one other masculine boy who appeared comfortable enough to give off some homosexual leanings.He had a beautiful body, a result of working out regularly at a nearby gym (not many kids did that). He was short and stocky and Andrew had read somewhere that physical types such as that were often well endowed . . . It might not have been true but it certainly added to the arousal factor providing for several happy orgasms. Gary (his name) made several offhand remarks which implied that physical togetherness was a distinct possibility. Despite that, Andrew could never quite bring himself to making an overt move. Maybe "it takes one to know one" was in play once again. Andrew just wished that he was more physically appealing. On the whole, his classmates were much more clean cut, had better skin and were more athletic. Mostly, it was still his ugly glasses that messed everything up for him. His mother couldn't have made a worse choice and it made him look absolutely "spooky". It surely didn't help his cause and with Gary he feared rejection along with embarrassment. Better to keep Gary in fantasyland and hope that something unexpected might happen.

So—his 13th year was a dry one sexually except for those solitary pleasures that came with his "hit parade" list inspiration along with the always pleasurable experience of going to school and enjoying the visuals. It kept him delightfully distracted although not to the extent of ignoring his schoolwork. And he always conducted himself in an acceptable manner. He was proper on the surface and was sure that none of his compatriots saw any ulterior motives in his casual give and take. Indeed, the back-and-forth communication gave him a few cheap thrills as well as some sense of sharing. Meanwhile, sex was becoming more of an obsession and he really couldn't shut off that part of him.

His luck was about to change! In January of his 14th year dear old dad decided to get out of town. He had retired with a nice nest egg and had had enough of cold winter weather. Some of his retiree friends had put him on to Florida. Dad had rightfully concluded that the warmer air might prove beneficial to his circulatory problems. So it was that in very short order Andrew would find himself in a local Florida high school. It would prove to be very different from what he had experienced in the Northeast. The student body was a genuine mix of types, some of whom might be described as "rednecks". That didn't bother Andrew; indeed there was something appealing about those rougher looks. In another reversal, the students in general were more open about their feelings and certainly more willing to experiment sexually. In the end, the move to Florida turned out to be largely fortuitous although it didn't seem that way at first. It was that old bugaboo of fearing the new. Just the thought of starting all over again at a new school was frightening enough. Even his dad would eventually realize that the school was not going to provide a good enough education. Although he didn't know it at the time, Andrew would eventually find himself in a very pleasant boarding school. But that was getting ahead of the story. Florida,though, would prove to be the link whereby homosexuality would forever rule his sexual "house". One very special boy would provide all the needed "ammunition" to fortify Andrew's need for continuing male companionship.

His name was Mark and Andrew had instinctively identified him as a real sexual possibility. He was one of the horny looking boys confused about his own sexual identity. It took very little effort on Andrew's part to open the conversation and to make it clear that they were both, figuratively speaking, groping. Quite a change from only a year ago when he dared not say a word. Now, all of a sudden, thoughts were out in the open and action was there for the taking. Andrew would later learn that these Florida boys were much less inhibited and more than willing to experiment.

So it was that Mark came into Andrew's life. Mark's demeanor gave off his questioning nature (more of "it takes one to know one"). A mutual attraction was certainly there although Andrew wondered whether this was all just part of the growing up process and that, like many of his classmates, his needs would soon shift to women. He didn't really think twice about it, looking upon experimenting as part of sorting things out. That didn't explain the intensity of the feelings that would soon develop between him and his new partner. Mark would turn out to be not only a great joy but, upon later reflection, the first love of his tender life. Up until that point, complete physical sharing had been absent. Now though there would not only be sharing but high levels of ecstasy and understanding as well. Andrew was a little bit surprised that he had registered so favorably with Mark (those ugly glasses again). Whatever—a signal was registered and Andrew sensed that good times were coming (anticipation was always lovely). Mark made it clear that his house was empty (dad was working and mom was socializing). The house was located on what might be described as the "wrong side of the tracks" but it was nice enough and Andrew couldn't have cared less about location. He just wanted some physicality. The plot had thickened over the course of several days. This gave Andrew more than enough time to ratchet up the excitement level. He had absolutely no worries about performing beyond premature ejaculation. Mostly, he just hoped that there would be some sharing going on. In the end, he would not be disappointed. In the end, he would not be disappointed. There was something particularly unique about Mark. He was so beautifully natural and uninhibited. It made the physical sharing with him so much more vital and,consequently, like nothing Andrew had ever before experienced. Just the bodily closeness between them felt so natural - as if it was always meant to be. It made for a certain excitement, the likeness of which was beyond anything Andrew had ever thought possible. It was, indeed, his "watershed" moment out of which all future sexual activity would take "center stage".

Andrew now had a new friend even though they didn't talk a great deal about it. Still, they would share many more moments of physicality. Beyond the sex, however, they had little in common and this somewhat limited their general conversation. Andrew's mom always stressed the avoidance of class distinctions and so, for Andrew, all that really mattered was the great sex, never mind the different social backgrounds. Andrew would like to have showed off his own more upscale lodgings but that was too risky as one or both of his parents seemed to always be at home. And, again, location didn't matter. There would be problems over time but these had nothing to do with location. Rather, the fault would lie with Andrew and his need to prove himself elsewhere. He was fickle and that was the basis for his main problem. Mark had been great but Andrew was beginning to think that it might be fun to experience others. He had conquered one and now wanted to move on to another (and maybe another after that). He had no idea where that had come from, only that he would later learn that it was all too common. Even his father had been guilty of stepping over the line. One night dad had left the nest and went on the "wrong side of the tracks" to indulge himself with a blue-collar lady. It had really upset the household and taught Andrew a lesson to the extent that sex outside of commitment was not a good formula for stability. In the case of Mark, there had been no commitments, just an understanding that what they shared was special. It did make for a great deal of confusion as Andrew knew that his parents had earmarked him for greater things. He would surely be expected to marry well and produce a brood that would include another namesake. All that, of course, was still in the future and he put it aside for the time being.

During that one year hiatus in Florida there would be two additional physical lookups although nothing as connected as had existed with Mark (mom always said that comparisons were odious). The other couplings more or less fell into the cheap thrills category and were not particularly fulfilling. They did, though, further strengthen Andrews attraction to other men, finding the male anatomy much more interesting. He hated the way that most of his classmates carried on about girls and the beauty of their physicality.

Changes were afoot! The end of the school year meant the end of the local high school for Andrew. Dad was now speaking from "on high", declaring that it was time to move on and get a better education. Andrew had long grown used to those declarations but there was nothing he could do about it. So—once again there would be adjustments to be made to a new environment where he would have to work to achieve some comfort in the midst of all this sexual confusion. A New England boarding school it would be—one of those "leafy" places where the upper classes sent their children to help them matriculate into highly ranked colleges.

The new school seemed okay on the surface. It was a lesser ranked private New England boarding school but that still meant that most students would later get a very good college education. The best part of it for Andrew was the fact that it was an all boy environment. Yet, he would have much preferred staying in Florida which was familiar territory. He nevertheless made peace with it although fearful that a boarding school environment might mean the end of his sexual adventures. In the end, he decided to put a positive spin on his new home. After all, an all male environment couldn't be that bad!! Others would surely complain about the lack of female companionship but that would only give him a sense of one "upmanship" with his peers. He would also now be part of a clean-cut, preppy environment which always held appeal. He might have found some attraction in the horny,blue collar types but the clean cutters would always predominate his thinking.

The school turned out to be a perfect fit. It was relatively small and Andrew came to realize that he could now be a bigger "fish" in a smaller pond. As expected, the "clean cutters" were in the majority but there was also a sprinkling of poorer breeds that made it more interesting. Andrew actually developed a pretty good gift of gab. Initially, sex remained in the background despite easy arousal over the visuals. Male fantasies were always close at hand and became particularly appealing when athletic contests were involved. One of the first things Andrew did was to volunteer as a reporter for the school newspaper. This gave him an entrée into the gymnasium for interviews with team members. There was further inspiration to be had when he joined Mr. Talbot's exercise class. This featured naked students, their privates hidden only by athletic supporters. This made things rather eye-popping.(for him at least). It seemed like an odd way to assemble the students but Andrew certainly wasn't complaining. Distractions like that were becoming all too frequent, sometimes to the detriment of his schoolwork. It also made him anxious for some sort of physical togetherness. He didn't know it at the time but relief would soon be on the way; in fact, right across the hall from his room. Andrew had a private room which was rare but certainly appreciated as Andrew really did need his privacy. As luck would have it, there was a student across from him who acted as if he might be a willing sexual accomplice. That boy was what might be described as a mixed breed—combining the best of "preppy" with blue-collar. He had big eyes and big hands and beautiful soft skin. Willingness was surely there and one night they agreed to meet after dark in Daniel's room. Daniel did turn out to be quite wonderful but then again almost anything would've been fine at that point. Andrew was just happy that he could roam at will over Daniel's body and bring him to climax. Over the course of the winter months they would meet several times—often in the offices of the school newspaper. And when spring arrived, the activity would switch to the outdoors. Andrew thought that that was particularly romantic although he sensed that Daniel was growing tired of the routine. Indeed, they did finally break it off when the school year came to an end.

Andrew really had little to complain about. He was older now, and still questioning his principal attraction to other boys which had only increased. He thought it was never going to go away and wished he could find a soulmate or at least one having similar experiences. It all remained quite problematic, mostly because those were difficult times (the 50's) to feel comfortable about homosexual acts. Making overtures to others of the same sex was risky. Later he would find college almost too grown-up, very spread out and just too unmanageable. He would also soon have to deal with the aging process and the loss of virginal looks. There had been something wonderful about youthful innocence but there was no stopping the clock.

College would pass in a blur! Strangely, Andrew was beginning to find some appeal in women who surrounded him during fraternity party events. Maybe he was moving away from his one way male attraction zone. In truth, he was probably mentally getting himself ready for parental marriage pressure. His parents had already started making noises about that. Of course, the emphasis had always been on a nice girl with good breeding. So, maybe all his mental gyrations were part of a long process and that he was a late bloomer. As usual, he wasn't totally honest to himself for he still found something very appealing about the male torso. Joining a fraternity also bred trouble in that there was constant pressure to conform to heterosexual dating procedures. A girl by your side was expected and conformist Andrew went along with the crowd. His first real date had been prearranged through another fraternity member. She would turn out to be a mistake on all counts. For starters, she was oversexed and demanding. Cheek to cheek dancing would never do for her. Andrew tried to be cool about it but was inwardly terrified. Of course, the more he resisted, the more she wanted. Andrew went along with a little petting but it did nothing for him. He did think that maybe what he needed was somebody a little softer, a little more gentle and certainly somebody he could dominate.

For the rest of his years in college he played the part—presenting his very straight and serious side to the majority. All the while he still remained on the alert for any male to male opportunities. In most cases, those he found particularly appealing were not available under any circumstances. He continued to keep up appearances by heterosexual dating but none of his dates were very successful (little arousal and certainly no feelings of passion). He was fortunate only in that men were not expected to go all the way. There was then no female pregnancy protection outlets and most of the guys didn't much care to stop in the heat of passion and slip on a condom. Besides, most girls still believed that the complete act was reserved for marriage. Thus, going all the way was not expected and for that Andrew gave genuine thanks. His fraternity brothers complained about the lack of sex outlets but Andrew took it easily in stride. He had heard tell of a homosexual cruising area and he actually once drove to check it out. He quickly turned around after spotting a police cruiser nearby.

The 2nd year of college brought with it a homosexual fraternity member. He would immediately recognize a kindred spirit in Gary. Poor Gary wasn't much to look at and was hyper nervous about everything. Still, he was a live male more than willing to participate in physical liaisons. Gary initially lived in a freshman dormitory with two other roommates so that get-togethers were not easy to come by. And the living quarters in the fraternity were also much too close for comfort. Besides, a good percentage of the brothers looked upon Gary as a "fruitcake" and, as such, hanging out with him was guilt by association. Indeed, Gary would never have been admitted to the fraternity in the first place save for pressure from the University to admit more members. So—Gary had been admitted but most members were not comfortable about it and Gary was certainly not "one of the boys". For Andrew,though, it was nice having another gay person around and eventually he and Andrew did have sex—in a car no less, coming back from another laughable heterosexual double date. It was nothing more than a quickie where they pulled off to the side of the road and did some hasty kissing and groping. It happened a few other times but as it turned out, that would be the extent of his college homosexual experiences. Aside from that, college was great despite the slim pickings sexually. Andrew did have a steady stream of roommates but they were all girl crazy. He did manage to develop a close friendship with a fellow fraternity brother who had the cute nickname of Woody. Andrew thought that Woody would've made a perfect life partner. He was intelligent and possessed an unusual degree of sensitivity. Sometimes he was so needy that he almost seemed to be "coming on" to Andrew although Andrew knew better. Still, it all aroused him and provided a great deal of masturbatory inspiration.

Upon graduation, Andrew moved to New York. He had gone through the job search process and decided that the "Big Apple" was the place for him. His father had now "stepped up to the plate" big-time, temporarily pushing Andrew into the world of finance. Andrew hated to be pushed and resented the authority figure despite, at the same time, wanting to please it. He was at least happy to be going to a big city, considering it a more likely place to find same-sex companionship. He would eventually find that, although it would not be easy since even in big cities there were limited meeting places as well as the constant threat of police entrapment. Initially, he moved in with two other recent college graduates who had advertised for a third roommate. Fortunately for Andrew, they held no physical attraction for him. Further, they both had serious girlfriends and largely kept to themselves. Andrew went to work in a bank training program and took an immediate dislike to the work assigned to him. It didn't take long for him to realize that he had made a bad vocational choice. Further, the pressure from the home front to find a steady girlfriend had been "amped up".

Andrew was quite flummoxed at first. Between job dissatisfactions and sexual question marks, he didn't quite know how to proceed. Basically, he knew that his attraction to other men was not going to go away and he rather suspected that at twenty-three years of age he was not going to grow out of his rampant homosexuality. On the other hand, he always wanted to keep the peace on the home front so perhaps there would be some way to compromise this situation and sprinkle a little joy all around. Bad idea! and it would later prove disastrous. At the time, though, he rationalized by telling himself that he hadn't really given heterosexuality much of a chance. Maybe he might find some limited satisfaction if he made a better effort. He had also read somewhere about bisexuality and maybe he could slot himself in that category and make everybody happy. It would also keep him in the mainstream and that counted for a lot. Then again, Andrew had no knowledge of the homosexual underworld and the sociability available for those who looked upon themselves as "different". Still, Andrew couldn't imagine limiting his social life exclusively to other gay men.

He was lucky! A perfect heterosexual situation came to his attention and was barely ten blocks away. Close at hand resided some former friends of his family. It just so happened that they had two daughters, one of whom was close to his age. His dad looked upon them as a rung below acceptability although Andrew didn't quite understand that. Their daughters had gone to private high schools and then on to top ranked colleges. Andrew was particularly interested in the blonde daughter closer to his age(If it can't be a blonde boy it had to be a blonde girl). She had also been dealing with diabetes from an early age which, for Andrew, meant less pressure for sex while maintaining full control of the relationship. As it all played out, there was an extended courting period during which there was little chance for sexual trial and error. Premarital sex was still a no no—at least for those on the proper "side of the tracks". There was some petting (sort of) and some deep kissing, none of which created any arousal. It now occurred to Andrew that sex with a woman was going to be a hurdle. In the meantime, he was getting some cheap thrills from the visuals at his job. One in particular stood out. He was a lovely blonde, pretty boy, a recent graduate of Yale, who gave out what Andrew thought were sexual innuendos. It would've been nice had there been some back and forth chemical attraction going on but Andrew was very unsure about that and hesitated making any overt moves. Holding back would happen a lot over the years and he often wondered how many opportunities he had missed. In this particular case, they were in a close working situation and stepping over the line might cause problems. But, the boy was a real tease sometimes—even suggesting sharing lunch together in his apartment (he lived nearby).

Andrew was surely in a terrible quandary. He was still dating his new girlfriend and seeing her once or twice a week. She had very outgoing and overly friendly parents and, in truth, he often enjoyed the family pleasures more than the lonely female companionship. Not a good sign although Andrew was quite sure that she represented his best opportunity in the heterosexual marriage stakes. Yet, male imagery still predominated. Beyond the blonde working buddy there were other lovely visuals of young men who passed before him every day—on the way to work, during lunch breaks and going up and down various office buildings. Looking at them and sizing them up became a daily ritual and one that was eagerly anticipated. Although he didn't know much about that world, fantasy thoughts continued to dominate.

He did finally get married although the marriage wasn't consummated until the morning after. The hangover horniness did the trick!! The wedding had concluded with a "blowout" party at which vast amounts of alcohol had been consumed. He gave thanks for that hangover sex drive since he would've been terribly embarrassed had he not been able to perform with his new bride. It had not been a particularly easy or comfortable event as the girl was a virgin resulting in some difficult penetration. He had nevertheless forged ahead and once the hymen had been pierced, the second and third times were much easier. Still, he was glad when it was all over, and, at the conclusion of the honeymoon, he judged that he had made a mistake. Yet, even knowing that, he was determined for the time being to make peace with his mistake.

His marriage worked for several years. The scenario played out much as he had formulated it. Two children were born and a suburban lifestyle was established. He had most surely chosen well in selecting a bride who was dependent on him on all matters—not just sex. The sex itself had largely "dried up" after giving birth—in large part because she felt that she had done her job and now needed to step back. All this coincided with Andrew's growing need for male companionship. It was only accentuated by his continuing interaction with his fair-haired training department buddy at work. The sexual teasing had only continued although once again

Andrew made no overt moves. All of this wasn't very helpful in terms of a satisfying marriage. Peace was maintained temporarily but Andrew suspected that it could change in an instant if the right male opportunity presented itself. In a certain sense he felt trapped and his immaturity didn't help matters. He had always accentuated the good things in life with himself at the center of the gratification scale. Work was nothing more than a necessity to support his gratification needs. Titles meant little to him except that they boosted his ego. Titles were a common enough occurrence within the bank structure and didn't mean much in the sense of the "big picture". They did, however, come with salary increases which would help fuel the pleasure principle. They also came with expense accounts that would prove to be a ready source of abuse. Spending other people's money provided him with multiple satisfactions. They gave impetus to living the high life while also accentuating his disrespect for authority. And should he wind up in a traveling post (he did), the pressures to perform on the home front would be lessened.

Looking back on it, he should've realized the changes were afoot. Like so many others, he got complacent about all the benefits and greedy for more. Much like a common criminal, there would be greater excesses that were foolhardy and bound to eventually catch up with him. They did, at least, lead him to discover the easy access to male sex. An article in a local newspaper caught his eye as it told him of the existence of gay meeting places—bars and meeting rooms that operated in urban centers. Many pleasures would follow and one particular incident would stand out at the center of the new course that he would soon be taking.

His name was Eric and they would meet in the nicest of places. It was one of those fancy resorts that Andrew had zeroed in on during the height of his expense account mania. Andrew had been slightly inebriated after an evening of entertaining customers in one of the resort's high priced restaurants. He was at the bar enjoying a nightcap and was in a true relax mode. He quite enjoyed watching the crowd but, then again, he never had much of a problem entertaining himself and rather enjoyed taking in all that was happening around him. Over the years, he had become rather good at being the life of his own party. It would often lead him to drink too much and on that particular evening entertaining customers had given him quite a head start. Much like his dad, he would always want more. At least his room was close at hand which made it easier to further indulge. The bar was crowded and as luck would have it, the only available seat was next to Eric. Andrew was not expecting much since past experiences with bar chatter had been uneventful and with a decidedly heterosexual bent. Eric would be different—very different. Intuitively, Andrew thought that Eric might be amenable to something more than small talk. Eric looked great (he had obviously taken care of his body) and he was very handsome with a full head of straw colored hair. Andrew could not have ordered up a better prospect. In very quick order, the chemistry was established and, joy of joys, they would be sharing each other physically. It was wonderful although Andrew quickly realized that he had a great deal to learn. As it turned out, Eric lived an exclusively gay lifestyle and would introduce Andrew to all that was involved in living that lifestyle. That evening with Eric went on for hours. Not much sleep what with so many cuddles and kisses and bodies embracing. There was something just totally natural and comfortable about it all and certainly the climaxes were like nothing he had ever previously experienced. They were so good, in fact, that Andrew knew that there was no going back, no settling down with his wife, or, for that matter, any wife.

In the space of a few short hours, Eric would become a much needed teacher and a passionate one at that. Eric obviously enjoyed guiding an ignorant soul that was the essence of Andrew. After that night, Andrew realized that he had a lot of catching up to do. He learned in much greater detail about the assorted gay meeting places and how to locate them. In time, the bars would hold a particular fascination for Andrew as the alcohol would lower resistance and inhibitions. This would make it much easier to find bed partners. In the 1960s and the 1970s those bars would be in out-of-the-way locations since caution was the byword. Of course, Andrew was cautious by nature and, besides, the risks seemed minimal when weighed against the possible results. Eric also told him about gay publications and directional guides along with phone hotlines that were available in every city of decent size. This would later beautifully mesh with Andrew's travel schedules. Soon, a pattern would develop whereby the first order of business was checking with the local hotline. The selection process was always relatively simple since choices were limited. He steered clear of the "old folks" places and had no interest in the leather crowd. His requirements were relatively simple. He only wanted a bedmate that, like himself, was young and decent looking and enjoyed cuddling.

Success quickly settled in and accessibility became more than he had ever imagined. In many ways, it was easier than making new female friends. The ladies were much more resistant to sexual acts and, at a minimum, required more sociability. Men tended to be "pleasure palaces" and went to gay bars with the express purpose of finding a one time bed partner. Andrew thought there was something exciting about the "hunt"— especially since in most places he had a distinct advantage. He was, after all, the new face in town and that alone triggered curiosity. He particularly enjoyed the Midwest boys as he found them much more honest than the big "city slickers". There was something really energizing about their "goofy" manners and their general honesty. In general, what you saw was what you got. They tended to be unencumbered with sophistication and that was lovely. Andrew would almost always connect although sometimes he would have to wait until the end of the evening. This sometimes played havoc with his next day business responsibilities but somehow he always managed to bounce back and carry forward properly with his working duties. He rather thought that perhaps the orgasmic pleasure of the night before had served to energize him and make him feel invincible, no matter what the task.

It was easy enough to imagine a perfect sexual world continuing without interruption. Andrew got quite comfortable with the routine (he always loved those routines).He only wished that he had become aware of it much earlier. Of course, it fed upon itself so that the more he got, the more he wanted. He did at least realize that this sort of activity was not a healthy long term proposition. Worse—it did not bode well for a future monogamous relationship. Yet, he carried on and, for the time being, at least, wallowed in the joys of reciprocal sex after years of living in a fantasy world.

One obvious conclusion to all of this was that there was no longer any doubt about his principal sexual orientation. There would be other diversions along the way but there would always be a need for physical sustenance from another male. It surely didn't bother him—quite the opposite as he got excited over the thrill of the chase. No longer could he imagine living a heterosexual lifestyle in the suburbs. Lots of people did that (his siblings being the prime examples) but it was never going to satisfy Andrew. He vowed to himself to move away from those preordained suburban groupies. This was going to involve some major changes. Indeed, it was going to be particularly difficult for Andrew as he hated surprises—especially those originated by himself. He was also by nature a peacemaker and a person who resisted unpleasantness and the use of harsh words. On the other hand, he couldn't continue living a lie about something as important as his sexuality. He had known a few friends who lived double lives in maintaining a heterosexual marriage for appearances while having male sexual adventures on the side. For Andrew, this was unacceptable and he needed to take steps sooner rather than later. Not for him would there be sex on the side. Somebody once told him about activity between men in commuting train stations before heading home to family. He couldn't imagine doing such a thing while appearing to most as a model heterosexual. Anonymous sex would never be really fulfilling. Homosexuality was still not acceptable to most, but there was enough of that going on so that he could center his social life around his gayness. Eric had given him a clear impression of New York City and the gay outlets there. Andrew was certain that he could easily move within all of this once he relocated from the suburbs. His mind was now whirling and plotting and there was a sense of excitement about it all. He moved cautiously at first. He made no announcements on the home front despite regarding it as a temporary base of operations. From suburbia he would take occasional forays into Manhattan late at night when he was properly "fueled". Thinking back on it later (he was still doing a lot of that) he realized how totally selfish he was at pleasuring himself. His frantic wife was not all that well to begin with and his leaving in the dead of night and not returning until dawn caused a great deal of heartache and worry. It was also fraught with danger in that he was behind the wheel of a car and prone to accident or arrest. Driving all that distance gave witness to the desperate needs that had built up inside of him. His wife, of course, had not an inkling of what he was doing. He would soon have to tell her as he was beginning to feel major guilt over his actions. The guilt was only magnified by the fact that his wife had done nothing to deserve this mistreatment. And her medical condition made Andrew's actions even more inappropriate. She genuinely loved him and, worse, had grown totally dependent on him for even minor needs. Her earlier sheltered life had come back to haunt her and now she was having serious problems just maintaining a household. She even dreaded going to the nearby supermarket. She could cope but only if Andrew was in her life providing mental and physical support. Now, all of that would be going away.

At least Andrew no longer had to concern himself with sexual pressures on the home front. A physical distance had been firmly established. His wife would often apologize for her lack of passion to which Andrew could only chuckle to himself and give thanks for not having to perform. Of course, lack of sex was no longer a part of the equation. Indeed, Andrew was having more sex than he had ever imagined possible. The trips into the city had increased and as this was the pre-AIDS time, there were plenty of lovely playmates anxious for pleasures. He did occasionally have the problem of waiting until closing time when his choices became more numerous. Andrew sometimes worried about what all this was doing to his health. But—those thoughts didn't linger for very long as he was still young and thought himself invincible. He was also catching up for lost time and was aware that before long his youthful appeal would disappear, making success with bed mates more difficult.

In short order he reached a state of desperation! In a very real sense sex activity had taken over his life and he was having trouble maintaining an even keel and keeping everything in some sort of proper perspective. So many thoughts running through his mind, none of which would be beneficial to his immediate family. His wife seemed to get more desperate by the hour and eventually reached a point where she would accept his outside activity so long as the suburban home was his center of operations. In other words, sex on the side was fine as long as she was properly looked after. This only gave him a greater sense of sadness and, in a perverse way, made the concept of staying home even more intolerable. He did eventually leave the homestead but it took longer than he had wished. Days turned into months and all this came at a time when his travel schedule increased. That translated into more physical pleasure. These sometimes led to overheated responses—phone calls and letters from bed partners expressing love and clamoring for repeat performances. Shortly after moving out of the suburban household, he took off on what amounted to a sexual vacation in the Netherlands. He had heard tell of the openness of the Dutch and he was not disappointed. Indeed, he became so entranced by one boy in Amsterdam, that he returned one week later to partake of further thrills. His gay world was surely continuing to expand and seemed endless to him. Sex was now in the forefront of everything. He was probably fortunate in never having any trouble in choosing a willing partner. Then again, he always had good intuition and stayed away from aggressive types. There were certainly troubles out there for those making poor choices, At one point he had read a newspaper article about a middle-aged gentleman who had a proclivity for young Puerto Rican boys and had paid with his life for it.

Not surprisingly, the upshot of his announcement that he was leaving home made for much turmoil but was not as bad as he had expected. He worried more about the children as they were quite attached to him and too young to fully understand what all this upheaval was about. The older one was the least affected as he had never gotten along with his mother in the first place. The younger one was the real cause for concern as he was more sensitive and more inclined to protect his mother. Still, Andrew never wavered and moved out in a hurry, establishing a new headquarters on the upper East side in Manhattan. This necessitated some financial wriggling as the suburban nest was sold and most of the proceeds were used to put his wife into a smaller home in a more downscale tract. That new home was at least close to the local school so the kids could find their way to the classrooms without parental guidance. This would later prove to be a controversial convenience but in the present it was a big factor in helping the stress level. The house was also conveniently located next to a shopping area which was easily maneuvered. Andrew was at least trying to make the best of it nearly impossible situation.

Living in the Big Apple only accentuated his already active sex life. No doubt he was lucky in being a creature of discipline for otherwise sex might have totally overtaken him. But—he never let it interfere with his work and when not traveling for business, limited sexual searches to the weekends. Of course, as already noted, "all bets were off" when it came to those road trips (generally two weeks out of every month)where work and pleasure mixed and "candles" were always burned on both ends. He was free now and pleased to be unshackled despite some guilt for the trail of hurt that he had left behind him. He did feel that he had juggled his responsibilities rather well-spreading concerns around in equal portions. He never once thought about turning back, just wished that he'd known himself better at an earlier age. Still, he felt that he had to made the best of a messy situation and that he had done the right thing in living his life as a gay man. He took a certain pride in finally living a life that was meant to be. Lots of zigs and zags en route but he had arrived although a torturous trip still lay ahead. And in the back of his mind, he sincerely hoped that he would eventually find a true soulmate to whom he could make a permanent commitment. Easy enough to articulate but like so many other things, the reality would be a very different matter. What appeared like simplicity on the surface would, in one instance, turn into a disaster, a result of his impaired judgment. He would also discover that his constant need for control and new faces would be the source of a little bit of "hell on earth" within his personal household.

HEALTH

HIS FATHER HAD BEEN A handball champion in 1925 Brooklyn. It wasn't quite as grand as it sounded as it had only limited populist appeal. Dad had also had some small success with squash racquets so there was some good hand/eye coordination in his makeup. It seemed almost fated that some of this talent would be passed on to Andrew. In this he was supported and encouraged by his father. Actually, supported was something of a a misnomer—pushed might have been a better verb. At any rate, Andrew had little choice for at age seven a racquet was placed firmly in his hands. At the time, tennis was the most accessible of the racquet sports. Even at an early age, Andrew could appreciate the good feelings that tennis exercise generated. Indeed, the good feelings were the only good part of it as Andrew didn't appreciate the nagging that came before. It was a clear sample of dad's "marching orders and exemplified Andrew's burgeoning resentment of all authority figures. He had no power over the decision making process and anger continued to "bubble" below the surface. Nevertheless, he followed orders and subjected himself to the toils and occasional traumas of his tennis world. This was a pastime in the beginning and not at the expense of his formal education. Rather, it came to dominate his free time with his dad berating him about the importance of it all. At the same time, his father also emphasized the sacrifices he himself was making in terms of lesson expenses that continued to pile up. Even at age 7, Andrew recognized the nonsense of this since his dad could easily afford the outlays. It was just another example of his father's dictating powers and the belief that he had all the answers. Andrew resented all the commands and knew instinctively that given time he would make his own "road map". For the time being, though, he had no choice but to follow orders as the alternatives were too frightening to contemplate. At least his body would appreciate the good vibrations given off by the exercise. He couldn't articulate any of this but, upon later reflection, it seemed to be the most sensible answer. It would also prove to be ironic in that his dad's pushing for athletic excellence would play a major part in giving Andrew a longer life. But, after his father had passed away, Andrew would become even more motivated to achieve success and, with it, a healthier body. Andrew could also point to the fact that behind every victory came the feeling that he was bettering his dad's earlier handball achievements.

Andrew couldn't remember a time when he didn't resent his dad (even long before his teenage years settled in). It was not just the pushing but also the fact that dad was always physically present. So—there were very strict rules about taking tennis lessons at specific times, tournaments that must be entered, and competitors on the local club level targeted for defeat. It seemed to be never-ending—his dad always staring at him from his ugly, oversized Cadillac convertible parked nearby. Later, there would be an angry critique at the dinner table in front of the assembled family. Andrew wanted to hide (or even run away) but he couldn't rationalize that with his underlying strong family values. At least rewards would come in the form of winning local tournaments. Even better, there was success to be found in regional and state competitions. Too bad that success didn't come with less criticism. Dad's comments actually got worse after he retired from the business world. It was then that Andrew became the new "pet project" on the activity calendar. It was almost a relief to return to school and out of his father's immediate sightline. Then again, school presented its own form of emotional difficulty. There were times when Andrew actually thought that his dad would be pleased if he made a career out of his tennis skills. Andrew had other ideas about that and, besides, at the time, there were limited financial rewards for playing on the tennis circuit. It did though, function as an ego booster and that was very important at the time. Fortunately, during his later high school years, he found an exercise mentor who preached the importance of exercise—especially to counteract bad habits (smoking and drinking). And, again, Andrew learned very early on that there was no "high" comparable to the one that came from a good exercise routine. He played tennis throughout his college years when surrounded by drinking and smoking. The exercise did allow him to get away with all that. A good workout washed away a multitude of sins. It was also good for his blood pressure for he had inherited that tendency and needed to watch out. Andrew also watched his diet, something very foreign to dad who had no intention of changing his bad eating habits. For dad, artery clogging would begin at an early age. In the 1950s and earlier, clogged arteries were an early death sentence—few medications were available and there were no reliable surgical procedures. For his dad, one problem would lead to another, including interrupting sleep patterns followed by the overuse of barbiturates. It surely had hastened a final breakdown and was a pattern that Andrew had no intention of following. Further destabilization for dad had resulted in his wife moving to a separate bedroom. All in all, a very sad nightmare and a major surprise for Andrew who always looked upon the homestead as a model mom-and-pop show. Still, as much as Andrew disagreed with his dad, the man's ending was a terribly sad affair. A once vital human being had become crippled whereby he could barely walk 100 yards without having to stop and catch his breath. The physical picture was also ugly in that the body had become sunken and barely recognizable. There was also the sadness of a father begging forgiveness for past mistakes. Quite a contrast to the man who had thrived on giving orders and maintaining control. The sadness was complicated only in that his father had no real idea of Andrew's motivations, much less his having to deal with his increasing need for male companionship. Andrew should have been more forthright but keeping the peace was much more important. Besides, Andrew knew that homosexuality would prove to be the ultimate sin in dad's eyes, maybe even leading to his being disowned.

The long decline of his dad had brought with it deep thoughts of health and longevity. Andrew respected life and very much enjoyed being amongst the living. Despite many difficulties, he had not once suffered from the pangs of depression. His sister had gone through a bad "patch" whereby she maintained that she couldn't cope (that overused expression!). In her case, it made little sense especially since she had been blessed with a rich husband and three intelligent, well behaved children who had grown up to make their parents proud. No such simple life for Andrew yet he had always appreciated his talents and his capabilities in properly dealing with problematic situations. And he always woke up each day and gave thanks while maintaining a positive attitude no matter what had transpired the day before. He did suffer those occasional down moments but his glass was always "half full". Much like Scarlett O'Hara, there would always be another day and he vowed to work hard at eliminating negatives. There were, nevertheless, bad habits that took some time to conquer. In this, the parental environment had played its part and contributed to smoking addiction as well as problems with alcohol. Both of those demons relaxed him, made him more outgoing and was the perfect elixir for his innate shyness. It had also been his soulmate during the sexual searching process. No doubt about it, he liked what alcohol and cigarettes did while at the same time being wary of them. Actually, it was more than wary. There was an element of terror underneath it all; the fear of becoming totally dependent. Fortunately, the good side of those fears was that he would be pulled more and more in the direction of athletic "highs" which were so much more rewarding.

As for his health, Andrew had been fortunate in his timing. As he entered middle-age, the blood pressure problem appeared and there were medications that could bring it under control. For some time, exercise had kept his blood pressure readings at acceptable levels. However, as age entered the picture, exercise no longer could be counted on to maintain control. So it was that prescription drugs would be ordered and much-needed, particularly since bad habits had continued. Over time he would really need them. And Andrew made very few concessions to his bad habits. The drinking stage largely retreated except for the usual weekend overindulgences. Andrew had long since admitted to himself that he had an addictive personality and that only a strong discipline had prevented him from any greater problems. At least he had enough sense to stay away from other, more dangerous stimulants. Still, there would be the occasional alcohol blackouts and, once, a dizzy spell on a subway platform that had sent him rushing to the doctor. He knew that he was treading a dangerous path but the power of alcohol to liberate him was just too strong to give up entirely. In the end, it would take a medical crisis to wake him up to the seriousness of his habit. That crisis came about when he woke up one morning with a raging fever. He initially thought that he had run afoul of some horrible infection. As a young boy, he was always relatively healthy—even to the extent that he avoided most common colds or wayward bugs, common things that would temporarily disable his peers. His mom was naturally happy about that although fearful that Andrew might be one of those people who, when he did get sick, became critical. He recalled one time having a 104° temperature and being delirious and so clogged up that he had required a steam machine to relieve his breathing. Frightening!, although, of course, he eventually revived without any lingering repercussions. His mom watched over him, hoping that he would remain a generally healthy soul. Indeed, her hopes were largely vindicated and, for the most part, he mostly remained uninfected. Still, when he did get even a cold, it seemed to be worse than anything others experienced. No simple stuffy noses for Andrew. Instead, infections would gravitate into his larynx or chest. He would be miserable for what seemed like forever and now with this latest infection, past experiences came to mind as he had chills that no heavy blanket seemed to alleviate. Strangely, the chills would go away for hours at a time and he seemed to be his old self. This "in and out" would go on for several days and eventually a sense of panic settled in. He did finally turn to the medics who subjected him to tests and confirmed that he had a strain of hepatitis. Sad news indeed! for he knew that quite often a diseased liver came with fatal implications.

For the first time in his relatively short life, Andrew had visions of mortality. Obviously, his promiscuity had been the culprit. It was all very scary—especially since his life to date had been largely crisis free. As such, he had never given much thought to any potential physical threats. He was aware of other sexually transmitted diseases but also knew that they could be treated with antibiotics. Hepatitis was another matter entirely and there wasn't much to be done beyond taking certain cortisone compounds and hoping for the best. The disease came in different varieties and in extreme cases could result in death. Fortunately, Andrew had been infected with a less serious strain although even with that, serious liver damage could result. Now with the threat of survival potentially at stake, Andrew intended to do all in his power to conquer the infection and return to some semblance of normality. This would require a long period of clean living, one that would involve staying away from alcohol for a minimum of one year. The old maxim of an "ill wind blowing some good" would be particularly appropriate in this case. As he "dried out", he came to realize more and more that his drinking had become borderline out-of-control. A nice little disciplined college boy had become a young adult seriously dependent on outside stimulants. It even reached the point where the standard Sunday hangover took several days of abstinence and exercise to clear out his system . . . And then during those business trips, the heavy intake would become a daily affair. Now, though, not so much as a watered-down glass of wine would be acceptable. Andrew seriously wondered if he would be able to function without it. Discipline did take over and by the second week he had to admit that he was feeling much better. It also made him vow to himself that never again would he allow drink to take such control over him. Future drinking, like so much else in his life, would be compartmentalized—a time and a place for everything. As it later played out, there would be several testing periods wherein he would go over an edge. Still, those moments would be the exception rather than the rule. During his year hiatus he stayed away from bars and depended more on pornographic films for entertainment and quick orgasmic pleasures. A long way from a real physical presence but it served the purpose and, best of all, it was healthy. Indeed, health had moved to the head of the line. Alcohol stayed out of his life for the allotted one year time frame. And when it returned, it was a slow process that was initially limited to a wine spritzer (awful stuff)—diluted wine and water. Moderation was the byword and this even included long stretches of total abstinence. He took some pride in this crucial discipline. Cigarettes, too, remained firmly entrenched although there had been much bad press that made it something of a death threat. He did find it awfully pleasant despite the frequent coughing fits and greater shortness of breath. He never thought much of lung cancer, wrongly believing that he was too young to get anything like that. Most people early on refused to believe in the evils of smoking—especially after seeing doctors advertising the benefits of one company versus another. Gradually, though, over the next decade or so, the bad news became even worse and with it a slow decline in the smoking population. Even his sister and brother gave it up—especially after horror graphics became more prevalent. No doubt some family friends had succumbed although he had never remembered any specifics. Andrew continued puffing away, yet another victim of his addictive personality. Eventually, he would come to his senses and surprise himself by giving it up" cold turkey". Before that, he did have exercise in his favor and probably was lucky in that there was little if any cancer in his family history. Even his dad in his later years had cut back to only the occasional cigarette—no more than 8 or 10 a week. It was a different story for Andrew who for the longest time consumed more than a pack every day and more on the weekends when he was socializing. When he came to his senses, he fully understood how bad it was—not only for the damage done within but the fact that smoke had a way of getting into everything so that the house/apartment was in a constant state of smoky smell.

As noted, Andrew did at least stay away from other mind altering drugs. He had tested the waters with a few snorts of cocaine and some marijuana but he didn't much care for the effects on his system. The cocaine kept him awake and "pot" made him silly and hungry. He found other hallucinogens frightening—especially after having read about suicide urges while on LSD. For Andrew, being in a more sober state allowed him to appreciate even more the importance of living. It was a great privilege, something he had heard on many occasions from his mother who had proclaimed this despite her own set of physical problems. She had never given in to her ailments and exhibited for him the importance of making the best of the short time on earth. Out of all the things he had inherited from his mom, that fact stood out as the best! He made many mistakes but he always held on to the concept of living and being optimistic about it as well. As such, good health became more and more to predominate his lifestyle and that was a very good thing indeed.

WORK

ANDREW WAS ON THE GO—IN transit as it were—but the reflections continued racing through his mind. That was happening more and more frequently as his senior years increased. He might still be working although this was somewhat ironic in that he had always had a poor work ethic, due, in part, to his general resentment of authority. Indeed, he had always been "savvy" about understanding himself and even better at tracing the source of his motivations. His privileged lifestyle had come with its own set of nightmares as he fought a steadily losing game with paternal domination. It had been a losing battle for years, one in which his innate hopes had no chance for even a partial victory. He could do little more than escape within himself. Being true to his feelings had little chance against dad's proclamations about all things relating to Andrew's future. Living under the same roof had been easy early on as children were not permitted to be seen or heard of until reaching what was defined as a communicative age (nine or ten years old). By then, dad had long since figured out what would be best for Andrew—a future already "set in stone". Marching orders would follow soon thereafter. To hear his dad tell It, his formula was guaranteed to result in a grand success. This left little room for Andrew's own feelings, leaving him at the mercy of what was expected of him. Even before reaching his teenage years, Andrew knew that he was different and needed to be his own master. So—he was in a constant state of flux despite having no say in what came next. Such was the stigma of being the first born and the namesake. Initially, Andrew felt uncomfortable in this "grooming" process. He also didn't appreciate being put on a pedestal and looked at as the so-called hope for the future. He felt largely ridiculous and knew instinctively that none of dad's wishes were going to come to pass. He also resented being pushed in directions in which he had no say—sort of a" taxation without representation" situation. At the same time, he had a strong bent about wanting to keep the peace and avoid anger and disagreements. This, he had gotten from his mother's side of the equation even though she stayed largely in the background. Andrew was just plain helpless in the face of dad's domination. He "boiled" inside and vowed to fight back whenever an opportunity presented itself. Early resentment displayed itself when he was barely thirteen. At that young age, he became something of a minor thief, stealing money from his father's bankroll (dad never carried a wallet). Andrew quickly realized that $10 could easily be snitched without dad ever being the wiser. He also did his best to avoid dad wherever possible. He was facilitated in this by his father disappearing for long stretches on business trips (no jet planes back then). He remembered how pleasant it was with just he and his mother at home and he wished that it could go on forever. Too bad that dad would eventually return and take up the cudgel with a new vengeance. Before long, dad's agenda for him would play its first role. Andrew would matriculate as a fifth-grade student in his father's former private high school. It was located at the end of a Brooklyn subway line in what seemed like the far reaches of never—never land (Fort Hamilton). The school was okay but best of all it got him out of the house for long stretches at a time. It was at that point that the first hints of male attraction entered the picture. He was probably lucky to have been born with a certain native intelligence. It enabled him to get through his schoolwork with little effort. Dad would grumble that his grades were not good enough but Andrew took this in stride and spent allot of time on acts of vandalism. These included shooting hairpins at strings of lights in the subway cars. He enjoyed angering his father over it while mom looked at it all as nothing more than childish acts of a little" devil". In short order, numerous other acts of deviltry would manifest themselves, up to and including throwing

46

mud pies off the roof of his penthouse apartment. Looking back on it, Andrew knew that he was getting some satisfaction by showing the world that he was not entirely helpless in the face of adult superiority. Life would have been so much easier had dad not been around but that was not to be and, so, there would be further anger displays—especially with Andrew's growing attraction towards other boys. The next step on dad's career planning board for the future was a private boarding school at the age of thirteen. School now would become even more complicated by the onset of puberty. Andrew never liked the school although was partially comforted by the fact that he was surrounded by boys. Despite all that, Andrew discovered a growing need for seclusion. He needed his own space to sort things out and to deal with his confusing identity. He also resented having been sent away without so much as a word in the decision making process. It only added" fuel" to the growing anger over dad's authority. For Andrew, there was no right of appeal and so he once again turned to hostile acts and displays of unreasonable actions—all of which would eventually land him in the office of the school psychiatrist. The doctor was not very helpful. Poor grades were one thing but stealing (from local commercial shops) and drinking were quite another matter." Bad seeds" tended to gravitate towards other "bad seeds" which only got Andrew in further trouble. Eventually (and thankfully) the school had had enough and Andrew was eventually dismissed.

Finally, there would be that new school, one much more to his liking. Dad had retreated(surprisingly) leaving mom ascendant in the decision-making process. At last, Andrew had some say in a matter—something that would never have been allowed had dad been running the show. It was a smaller school and Andrew quickly realized that he was a much better "big fish in a little pond". Needless to say, His father would have much preferred locating him in a larger school with a better reputation. Fortunately for Andrew, larger, more prestigious institutions wanted no part of him. The decision played out brilliantly. He would become a minor star, eventually giving the valedictorian address at graduation. His dad was in total amazement and nothing pleased Andrew more than to watch the stunned expression on his father's face.

Of course, dad was not about to abdicate his "throne". A new decision was lurking on the question of college. Times had changed but not for dad who had grown up during a time when children went to work upon graduation from high school. Also, It was easier for his father since he was expected to enter the family business. Not so for Andrew as there no longer was a family business and times now called for a college degree if one expected to have a successful adult career. Even the girls were "hopping" on the education bandwagon. Once again mom made her presence known by insisting that Andrew needed four years of higher education. And once again dad actually backed off with the choice left largely in Andrew's hands. Andrew made a good choice, matriculating at a university that would lead to his election to the Cum Laude Society. It would also prove to be the best, most rewarding four years of his so far short existence.

Those joyous four years would allow for some breathing space before "dear old dad" would once again exert himself. By now, mom had retreated to the sidelines but Andrew would be ever thankful for the new lease on life that she had provided. Dad had stayed largely in the background save for his constant harping on the respect for money. He had made it very clear that Andrew was not getting a free ride in terms of incidental college expenses. This meant working a summer job to cover costs outside of regular tuition. So—while most of his college friends were enjoying themselves, Andrew was frantically working an eight hour job to provide him with "fun" money. His father may have weakened somewhat in his later years but he continued to be a commanding presence. Staying in the background for very long was never an option. Yet, as long as there was college and summer work, he would say little. As it developed, he was simply biding his time until graduation approached and the question of post college employment came to the fore.

At the time, Andrew was giving serious consideration to a teaching career. His last two years of high school had been so pleasant that he saw himself "leading the charge" of helping students who needed a good mentor. It would not have sat well with his father. Indeed, he couldn't imagine anything more diametrically opposed to his father's philosophy. Dad could only understand one thing and that was his namesake becoming a successful capitalist. Andrew didn't much care about that; indeed, he never wanted to please his father in any manner. For dad, teaching was the lowest rung on the entrepreneurial ladder. Andrew made several teaching inquiries but nothing appealing turned up. Once again, he was in a quandary. He wanted to go off on his own but also didn't want to cause a "ruckus" on the home front. In the end, he and his father reached a compromise of sorts. Andrew agreed to try the business world but would move on in a different direction if he found that world lacking. This was not a good way to start supporting himself since he was against the whole project in the first place.

Indeed, almost from the beginning, he knew that he had made a mistake. His initial effort had led him to a position as a trainee within a large New York City bank. This work centered in the Credit Department with responsibilities for analyzing financial statements. Andrew had never been much of a math student so spending days on end looking at figures was something akin to the ultimate disaster. He also didn't appreciate the office politics that were always present. The senior officers were largely Ivy League graduates(Yale predominated) who made little room for "outsiders" There was only one major compensation for all of this and that was that lovely Yale graduate who befriended him while making what seemed like sexual innuendos. Eventually, any decisions were taken out of Andrew's hands as the bank sold out to a much bigger institution which would deem Andrew expendable.

Andrew was quite happy to be set adrift and away from all those financial figures. He was in no rush to get re-employed and could afford to do that thanks to the state Unemployment Agency. Surprisingly, his dad turned out to be sympathetic, blaming Andrew's unemployment on the merger fever that was then in vogue. After several months, the schemer in Andrew rose to the occasion, pleading with his father to use his connections in possibly finding him some more suitable form of employment. Dad not only went "to bat" for him but, in essence, got him a new job compliments of one of his "gurus" who worked for another large New York City bank. The new job would have him selling investment services and it would lead to his appointment as a full Vice President. Too bad that Andrew didn't handle his rarefied status in a more proper manner as it would turn out to be be the high point of his long career earning power. He stupidly took advantage of expense accounts and the use of forbidden first-class air travel, looking upon his senior position as a carte blanche to do whatever he liked. This even included dinner treats for potential sexual playmates. There was little question that his ego needed continual stroking and unlimited financial transgressions made him feel on top of the world. Yet, it was only a matter of time before all that dissipation would catch up with him. A new financial efficiency expert would "sweep" him right out the door. Andrew was humiliated despite understanding that he had been in the wrong. Worse—he was unable to collect unemployment as disbursements were not permitted for those who had been separated for cause.

Earlier, his dad had passed away and Andrew gave a small measure of thanks that dad was not around to witness the shame of it all. Then again, maybe dad would've been able to work his magic once again. This was doubtful as Andrew turned to his mom for sympathy. He told her that it was the bank's fault, emphasizing that they had adopted a double standard that had snared him. This was all "gobbledygook" but it helped soothe his mother's feelings—a mother who constantly worried about him.

He got a break! It would eventually be only an interim "gig" that would prove to be a perfect fit for Andrew's continual need to be the ringmaster. An associate from college days had risen in the ranks of one of those old-line, blue blood firms. That institution was looking for an investment adviser to help them deal with institutional customers. It perfectly complemented what Andrew had been doing at the bank. His past transgressions were waved away largely because the brokerage firm was in real need and Andrew fit that need perfectly. Also, the stock market at the time had been "boiling" forward and little attention was being paid to dubious expense mistakes. Indeed, Andrew would be welcomed aboard with open arms and, as he quickly discovered, larceny available in his new position was even more blatant than what had existed at the bank. No lessons learned as the appeal for taking advantage was just too easy. All of the higher ups wallowed in their own fiefdoms and couldn't care less about Andrew's wayward expense "chits". This went on for the better part of a year until the "boiling" stock market turned to "ice". Much like the bank, efficiency experts came on board leading to the dismissal of many back-office people along with people like Andrew who were deemed extraneous. Another "gravy train" would thus come to an end, although, in this instance, he could at least salvage unemployment benefits. It helped dull the pain of his reduced comfort level. More explanations to mom followed.

She was beginning to wonder if Andrew was ever going to straighten himself out and steer a more normal upward path.

What next? Andrew was caught up in a web of confusion, none of which was helped by the passing of his mom which had made him an orphan. He missed her more than even he had anticipated. Her judgment was always sound. She made practical sense and provided him with some semblance of peace. However, that semblance of peace was proving to be more elusive than he had ever imagined and his confusing sex life was not helping at all. He had always told himself that identifying his true sexual orientation would make settling down an easy affair. He was totally naïve in believing that—especially since he had always been attracted to creative types who were often unstable. Also, for the time being he had no intention of remaining monogamous. On the other hand, he could not imagine agreeing to an open relationship in that it ran counter to his sense of family. So—he thought that he might have it both ways i.e. settling down with a lover while telling himself that cheating on business trips didn't count. He did take on a lover, but at the same time he always seemed to be in the process of falling in love with another. This happened mostly on the West Coast which seemed to be infiltrated with blonde, blue-eyed, baby faced young souls looking for opposites. He eventually grew to look forward to those trips as his partner of choice turned out to be a terrible problem case in all things mental and physical.

It would have been a perfect time for Andrew to have become a teacher. After all, his dad was now no longer around to protest such a move and his mom, had she been alive, would have given her blessings on such a move. He also could've done it easily from a financial standpoint as mom had left him with substantial assets. It was a major windfall and with proper management, would have provided comfort while he sorted out various teaching options. Unfortunately, Andrew was still in a foolhardy stage and not prone to make much sense when it came to money. Additionally, he was not a good captain of his own ship as he was still dealing with a wounded ego. For a short time, at least, he did find himself in a lovely position with his newfound wealth making him the great "ruler of his empire". It would not last as foolishness would eventually win out. Good times,though, did last for several years despite occasional big gulps of expense. He "played" for the first six months without even thinking about work. Instead, he set off on another grand sexual tour of Europe. All of this on first-class air travel and fashionable hotels. He thought that he could never get enough of those free-spirited males without any hangups about their sexual orientation. It was a breath of fresh air whose memories would stay with him for the rest of his life. He felt only mildly guilty leaving his so-called lover behind. That boy had never been able to pull himself together which lessened any respect Andrew might have had for him. A little bit of rationalization but it helped put his mind at ease. Upon his return, Andrew would enter into an occupation that initially worked well on his ego but would later be the root cause of financial disaster. Hard lessons would be learned but costly mistakes would take years to straighten out.

Only Andrew could devise an expensive way to crown both his ego while, hopefully, making a financial success out of him. Foolishly, he decided on what many thought the biggest financial gamble of them all. There had been untold warnings and the threat of very bad odds but Andrew persevered and now looked upon himself as the next big restaurant success story. Eating out had always been a big part of his life. And during his expense account years, he would always make a point of seeking out the best eatery, never mind the price. In the beginning, this was a normal operating procedure while working at the bank and brokerage house(somebody else was paying). Gradually, though, expense accounts would be better scrutinized and limits established. Of course, Andrew looked upon himself as above all that and, for a time, had gotten more creative about "stepping around" spending limitations. Eating out had been one of the major points of disagreement in his parents married life. Dad never wanted to eat out and his mom had to make strategic plans just to get herself to a restaurant. As his father became more debilitated, they stayed home even on the so-called maid's night out (usually Thursdays). Mom had lots of skills but cooking was not one of them. Andrew really enjoyed eating out and as he settled into the New York life, he made a point of going out with some frequency. In time, he would establish favorites whereby he would become quite familiar with the staff. These conversations only fueled his interest in establishing a restaurant of his own. In one particular instance, lengthy discussions with the chef at an upscale bistro became quite animated. As luck would have it (bad luck as it turned out) the chef had been looking to operate his own kitchen. Dreams of success now became the modus operandi as a bad idea moved towards fruition. The chef would later display a volatile disposition that would create havoc with the rest of the staff. Like so many others, Andrew knew little about the business and the high failure rate. Another lesson was about to be learned the hard way—real hard in this instance as losses would decimate most of Andrew's inheritance. Yet, in the beginning, problems were all in the future as he initially rhapsodized about the glory of success as a restauranteur. He tried to be careful—carefully staking out what he thought would be the most advantageous neighborhood. Unfortunately, the "cheapskate" side of his nature led to his turning down what would've been the most advantageous location. He thought the rent too high despite the busy nature of that particular N.Y. area (Columbus Avenue in the 70s). He did finally decide on the upper East side (way East) in an area filled with high-rise apartments but lacking any good restaurants. He would later learn that most of those people wanted to get out of the area when they ate out.

He did at least get one break. He made a very economical arrangement with a neighborhood construction firm looking for business. He was also able to purchase secondhand kitchen equipment (other restaurants having gone out of business). But, he made a bad mistake in limiting advertising and floral arrangements as well as "flip-flopping" about the target audience. Initially, the push had a decidedly gay flavor. When that failed to fill the seats (especially during the week) he reversed course and made a bigger push for a mixed audience. Confusion reigned! He also had to contend with heavy-handed bartenders frequently giving away drinks. The only really wise step he took was to make room for entertainment. He hired a piano player with a light touch that attracted a small celebrity group and they would help keep the restaurant "afloat" for almost two years.

Andrew was now a three-time loser with a very bad track record. It was inconceivable that he had allowed himself to wiggle into such a dead-end position. Only his native optimism kept him viably engaged in moving forward. What next? He had no options in the banking and brokerage field. Additionally, his entrepreneur adventure might be admirable to some but he would soon learn that many companies were fearful about taking on such a person. He found employers thinking that once a boss, always a

53

boss. And bosses often didn't enjoy taking orders from others.(or so they thought) Nevertheless, Andrew put a resume together that he thought would have wide popular appeal. He presented himself as the ultimate salesman with a strong ability to work with others. At least the economy was slowly coming out of the doldrums with classified advertisements on the increase. He sent his resume out to anything that made sense but initially got no response. He tried to be philosophical but, underneath, he was dealing with a strong sense of panic. However, he didn't change his social habits (he should have) and carried on much as he had always done (weekend revelries). In other words,he was as foolish as ever and gave up little while telling himself that something workable was just around the corner.

He did finally get a "nibble". It was, however, far removed from anything involving upward mobility. He would soon find himself trapped in an office with bosses on either side of him—physically so close that they could easily eavesdrop on every phone conversation. He supposed that it was appropriate punishment for someone like himself who had long resented authority figures. It was an employment agency that dealt mostly with clerical level employees but also had a small division that dealt with higher-level placements. These would be countrywide bank Trust Department officers who might be coaxed into taking new jobs. Sort of a poor man's executive recruitment operation. It was a commissioned job that looked easy enough on the surface. In truth, it was anything but, although Andrew, as usual, saw nothing but dollar signs flowing in his direction. Once again he would be sorely disillusioned, the office layout being only the first piece of the disillusionment puzzle. In addition to the physical closeness of management, six other desks shared the rather small space giving off a sense of a stock market "boiler room". Then there were the managers themselves, both having Anglicized names that covered their Jewish heritage. Andrew would later discover that their original names were so ugly that they warranted alteration. Andrew's immediate boss suffered from occasional migraine headaches which would result in spurts of temper that were inappropriate. Andrew did manage to keep himself afloat by a monthly draw which was nothing more than a company loan. Of course, he was expected to cover those advancements through placement commissions but, much like credit cards, the bigger the hole, the harder it was to get out. He did give it his "all" but had poor results. It would take most of his strength to remain optimistic in the face of what would turn out to be a temporary vocation. It was complete frustration from the very beginning. So many times placements would seem to be at his fingertips and then for one crazy reason or another they would fail to materialize and he would have to start all over again. Moving candidates from one job to another was difficult at best since most candidates were not adventuresome and often had wives and children who did not approve of making changes. "Roadblocks" were everywhere, causing further damage to his already weakened ego. On top of everything else, he was looked upon as an Ivy League star who was expected to do great things. This only added pressure that made him feel worse about his low production results. He could at least give thanks for one new positive that had entered his life. During the dreadful summer that his restaurant closed he had made a very fortuitous chance meeting that would lead to a life partnership. That sweet little blonde boy was the perfect antidote to all the bad that was twisting around inside him. Andrew had never believed in divine intervention but, in a strange way, it seemed as if somebody or something was looking after him and constantly giving him another chance. His new relationship was the one positive in his "comfort house". Through all of his vocational upset he finally thought that he was in love. In addition, his new attachment came with a working income that far exceeded anything he could ever hope for in his recruitment world. Overnight, a beautiful new boy had arrived and came with enough income to support them as a couple.

Now that he had some backup, he could comfortably move on and start a new vocation—one that would finally take advantage of Andrew's proven ability with a racquet. His blond "Adonis" suggested that he utilize his talents by becoming a full-time squash teaching professional. No more office and no more business world that he had come to resent. Within a week he had left the executive recruitment people and set out to explore his new athletic world. However, once again he was unable to collect unemployment as he had resigned of his own volition. That was okay as he had a strong cheering section at home—one that actually believed in him more than he believed in himself. He and his new love quickly became a team and, as soul mates, it gave him a greater sense of security in what was still an uncertain world. He was anxious about moving into a new athletic "world" while also wanting to settle in as quickly as possible. For a change, he gave thanks to his father for giving him the good hand/eye coordination that had played a large part in his racquet success. He was nevertheless glad that dad was no longer around to pester him. He was now able to pick and choose, beholden to no one but himself. Even better, he could now actually do something that he was good at and operate freely without any outside direction.

It was not going to be easy as the teaching world of squash racquets was a tight knit fraternity with many teaching pros holding down longtime positions. At least he had the growing popularity of the sport in his favor. Early on, squash had been largely confined to Ivy League institutions. Now, however, the popularity of the sport had grown so that even lesser-ranked schools were building squash facilities. New York City's private clubs were also feeling the pressure to expand. Almost overnight, new adherents were looking for racquet outlets. It seemed as if new clubs were popping up everywhere while tending to be more democratic and open to all those willing to pay a price for use. The older, more established clubs, tended to look scornfully on the upstarts although had to admit that all the new action was good for competition. The older places attracted the better players but neophytes were usually much more upwardly mobile. All this increasing activity and new venues helped Andrew in his search for a place amongst the teaching populace. Still, he wished that he could locate himself in the more established places as they tended to pay much higher salaries. He gave up on that right away as those clubs had long time employees who were not going anywhere. Still, once again he had dreams of glory and, sure enough, these would be sorely misplaced. Initially, though, he did get lucky! A mere fifteen blocks to the north of his new love nest was a club that had just opened its doors. He had come upon it one day as he took to his bike on an exercise jaunt. There it was, flags flying on every floor as if to announce to the world that it was the latest in all things athletic. Once inside, that proved to be largely the case—floors of weights and exercise machines, along with squash and racquetball courts (even a rooftop swimming pool). On the surface, it was mind-boggling and almost too good to be true. Visions of success swirled around him. He only hoped that he would prove to be up to the task were the job to be offered (it would be). After all, he was no longer in his prime being in his 40s and no longer a threat to those twenty year-olds who rudely dismissed him on those few occasions when they did battle. He could certainly still compete on an older age level and rather thought that, for the most part, teaching would be easy enough. Still, his hips were starting to bother him as the start and stop action was wearing them down. (A couple of compatriots had already had hip replacements). In the end, he gave it little thought. Basically, he was too excited about that. He was also excited by the sale of his upper East side co-op and the purchase of a downtown loft-sort of a honeymoon home for he and his new lover. All signals were go as he found himself happy on all counts.

His new workload would turn into a major disappointment. It was a contract widely beneficial to the owners and not respectful of Andrew's talents. He had no complaints about the physical plant as both the squash and racquetball courts were top-of-the-line. There was a young female manager on racquet duty who also supervised the reception desk. From what he could gleam, she was being paid a hefty salary on top of her lesson fees. No such arrangement for Andrew who would be expected to work the front desk while also being responsible for the squash activity. The desk clerk salary was barely above the minimum wage although Andrew could take up teaching chores when the front desk was not overly busy. (He could also keep all lesson monies). It was a win—win for the club in that they had a responsible official on duty without having to worry about costing them very much. At first, racquetball activity was busy while little was going on with the squash courts. Andrew was sure that he could make a go of it, visualizing busy courts and good lesson income. The challenge of that excited him and for a brief period of time he found himself in the spotlight. Management was helpful to the extent that they distributed neighborhood flyers announcing his arrival and availability. They also spent some money joining the New York City squash racquet leagues. Unfortunately, the club was located in a part of the city that had a high concentration of artists who tended not to be athletically inclined. It only made Andrew's job more difficult and, in the end, would not be financially rewarding. Initially, he managed to generate a few lessons but they were largely with older residents who took it up on a lark. There were some kids and celebrities in the mix but, overall, he generated only a few lessons—hardly the stuff of a living wage, much less a comfortable lifestyle. Frustrating! and it certainly didn't mix with Andrew's impatience as well as his belief in his teaching skills. He quickly wondered whether or not he was on another path with a bad ending.

Andrew had always been spoiled! Good food, comfortable surroundings and high-class friends had predominated. Even through continuing lean times, he had been able to maintain some facet of a comfortable living. Now, once again, those comforts would be threatened. His blonde beauty had decided that it was time to exit the retail world which, for him, was not a proper showcase for his innate creative talents. So—a new twist had been introduced at a time when Andrew had counted on his lover's salary to tide them over while Andrew struggled to make a go in his new exercise world. After leaving the retail world, lover boy had decided to go into business with a local artist to supply the New York City corporate world with art to place on the walls of their scattered offices. It seemed like a grand idea on the surface but it needed serious organization and that was not to be. Almost overnight, a good salary had disappeared (no unemployment benefits) and, worse, reserve funds had been appropriated to fund the startup. Andrew's comfort zone was wounded and overnight the security blanket vanished. Andrew had no intention of limiting the good times and they continued much as they always had—drinking and eating out and spending many hours at the theater. He largely wished away the problems believing that he had reached the" promised land". (Self-delusion again). He would often look in the mirror and congratulate himself on all the good that had come into his life. People at the Health Club were always telling him how much they envied his position in doing what he wanted. It satisfied his ego temporarily and dreams of glory became more prevalent with alcohol in his system. Last call drinking opportunities were always utilized and were a constant source of trouble. Unacceptable behavior would predominate and was particularly nonsensical in that he had a beautiful lover at his side. Almost like magic, one night stands would come into the picture and were not healthy for the long-term relationship that he had always wanted.

Of course, he knew all too well that relationships were never perfect. He took responsibility for his actions which, to his mind, were providing some release from their tenuous financial state. He and his partner were generating little income and refusing to alter their lifestyle and it was leading them down a "slippery slope". Andrew had quickly come to realize that the Health Club was never going to provide him with a living wage. He was feeling great and enjoying himself but lessons were providing only scattered returns. He had no star students or even ones with potential. He did reach out to a neighborhood elementary school where he conducted after school group lessons. Unfortunately for him, the children looked at it all as something of a joke and spent more time hitting each other than paying any attention to the rules of the game. The whole exercise also didn't add much to the bottom line. As the expenses mounted and the future remained in doubt, the criminal element once again came into the picture. Andrew's lover had also finally gone in a different direction, getting a real estate license and joining a local firm with a strong reputation in the downtown community. Initially, the real estate market had been strong but that soon changed as the economy in general slipped into the doldrums. Almost overnight, another panic scenario developed with Andrew fearful of losing the little that remained of their "nest egg".It needed replenishment and It didn't take long for him to realize that the front desk at the health club generated substantial cash sums from the fees collected for the use of the racquet courts.Late night hours(after 8 PM) were busy and a source of lucrative funds.

Andrew had always considered himself beyond criminal suspicion, presenting himself as the upright vision of the serious athletic teacher. Management also looked upon him as a wealthy "straight shooter"—a socially connected, upstanding citizen. The truth was very different from that, thus proving once again that appearances can be deceiving. It would be easy enough to cover the taking of funds from the front desk and he rationalized that action by telling himself that he deserved better and that he was being ill treated by the management.

The stealing was quite easy. Like so many criminals before and after him, the taking would increase over time as "greed" became the operative word. There was also a certain simplicity to it as nighttime players would often arrive without reservations and would pay by cash. So, Andrew could assign a court and pocket the proceeds. He quickly discovered that $50-$100 a night was easy. Each night he would return home to add to his rapidly increasing" pile" of paper money. It would prove to be more than enough for their social life while avoiding the use of credit cards. Much as he had stolen from his father, he took a certain pleasure in spending money that did not rightfully belong to him. Again, it was all part and parcel of that resentment of authority.It was not going to avoid their eventual day of financial reckoning but it bought time. In the end, it was all a futile exercise. In truth, he and his beauty boy needed to alter their lifestyle and be more responsible. Unfortunately, any thought of that was ignored at the time and the high living continued. Andrew also remained highly sexed and too often would take advantage of sexual diversions. All this heightened sexual activity was further stimulated by his job and the presence of young athletes both in and out of the locker room. Much as before, he still wanted it both ways—a partner forever, along with a little fun on the side.

His boldness on the criminal front eventually became more risky. As such, racquet courts that had been booked were now reported as canceled even though they were being utilized. He should have stopped after several close calls but, instead, laid low for only a few days and then resumed his misbegotten ways. It was a game for him and there was little guilt on his part. It lasted for a whole year and cost the club many thousands of dollars. He wasn't proud of what he was doing although certainly enjoyed the benefits. Unfortunately for him and much like his banking fiasco, an outside auditor would be the source of his demise. The club was doing well, membership was up, and the use of the upstairs fitness equipment had increased tenfold. The real question mark was the court income which had flattened after years of steady growth. "Red flags" were raised and greater attention was now going to be paid to the front desk and those employees directly related to court rentals. This was more than enough to jangle Andrew's nervous system—especially when it was decided that all employees would be subjected to a lie detector test. It might not hold up in a court of law but a bad finding would be a major black mark and an easy excuse to have him replaced. As the time of the test approach, Andrew found himself even more agitated. He had, of course, put an immediate stop to the thievery while also trying to maintain a calm posture. He still rationalized his actions by telling himself that his actions were a "tip" in lieu of a higher salary. Rationalization of the highest order but it helped calm him down and, hopefully, made him less prone to the zigs and zags of the detection machine. Calming thoughts and a small dose of valium would prove successful and for that he would breathe a big sigh of relief.

The trauma of it all cleansed his soul—at least for a short time. Much like his youthful deviltry, he vowed to renounce his wrong footed ways.Unfortunately, that wasn't going to solve the money shortages, to say nothing of supporting their generous lifestyle. He had become so beholden to his lover that he would essentially do anything to please him. That damned ego still needed affirmation! It was the root of so many inexcusable actions and try as he might, it was always a sad part of him. Life had been a continuing battle without any positive resolutions. And, the situation was about to get much worse—at least from a financial standpoint. The once" healthy" Health Club bankroll was quickly disappearing, thus returning them to being dependent on two very small incomes. He also still had two sons to educate although, thankfully, he had set funds aside to get them through college.Fortunately, the downtown apartment was owned free and clear and could be a source of additional funds—funds that would be needed as their high life continued unabated. Within a few months, they finally turned to a local banker for assistance. As such, free and clear would no longer apply to their condo as they sought a home equity loan. There would be a problem with obtaining that loan in that their combined income was not sufficient to pay down the principal. Both of their jobs had small fixed salaries and were dependent on sources that might or might not happen. A stagnant real estate market wasn't helping their cause even though the downtown area was attracting more people. The lenders also didn't like their personal situation(male partners were often unstable!) but were willing to make a small loan, albeit at a high rate of interest. At that point, bankers held all the trump cards and there wasn't anything they could do about it. The apartment had been assessed at $250,000 but the lending officer was not prepared to lend anything beyond $30,000. Andrew knew they were a bad credit risk and, worse, that the $30,000 was only a stopgap measure and was nothing more than buying them a little time. "Pollyanna" still ruled the day. As Andrew imagined "lover boy" soon making enough sales to satisfy their indebtedness. If anything was going to happen, it would have to be his partner as Andrew could never count on lessons to make any major financial contribution. Unfortunately, reality would soon intrude as the real estate market was not cooperating. Several so-called sure things advanced to a serious level but then fell apart at the last minute.

Initially, it was easy enough to cover the monthly bank payments. In effect, they used a portion of the initial loan to write checks in a timely fashion. This was not a good idea as they would soon be up against the law of diminishing returns. Income was the needed element and the poor outlook for that made for a greater sense of desperation. There were moments when Andrew thought of seeking out a new, rich lover. Indeed, shortly after the bank loan was granted, there was a particularly onerous patch of sexual transgression on his part. None of it made any sense beyond creating a tenuous atmosphere on the home front. There was always a steady stream of young boys looking for "fresh blood" but he always judged most of them as being too unstable. Besides, his heart was committed to what he had. Maybe his Scottish sense of family had reasserted itself. Whatever it was, he had no intention of moving on in a new direction partner wise. For better or worse, he intended to stay put as their troublesome life continued to unfold. Thank God for his optimistic nature and his continuing belief that good things were just around the corner.

It was a dubious hope, dependent solely on a turnaround in the real estate market. It was a market that was floundering even more and unlikely to change in the short term. Andrew continued as the master of self-delusion, always believing that good news was just around the corner. Even the stock market was giving off bad signals, making matters even worse. He never once blamed himself, taking it out on others when what was needed was a reality check. He had been lucky all along, getting bailed out when all seemed lost. Now he was on a downward spiral once again and was proving to be a poor" cheerleader" about it all. He needed to be much more decisive! Instead, his bad ego had let him down again and instead of taking command, he retreated by always wanting to please while falsely believing that salvation lay just around the corner. The real estate market was going nowhere and questioning his lover about it only created a nasty temper as deals continued to fall apart. As the months slipped by, Andrew's probing became more insistent and that only created a more turbulent home front.

There were other complications as well! Andrew still had financial responsibilities for his sons. He had no intention of abdicating these tasks but they had become a continuing burden as he and his lover settled into their new lifestyle. Andrew was determined to avoid a repeat of the alienation that had been experienced in his own childhood. As such, he worked hard at maintaining honest communication with them, emphasizing that he would always be available for them. Of course, conditions had radically changed since Andrew's youth. Alcohol had been a big problem for him but now other drugs had entered the picture and both of the boys had become involved with them. Andrew had frequent dreams of watching his sons grow up to become successful adults but that "balloon" was quickly deflated. For starters, his oldest son was not particularly bright and took three schools to earn his high school diploma and, as an adult, the boy would wander from one job to another. As for his younger son, he would early on exhibit signs of chemical addiction that would lead to an early death. Those sad end results would come much later and Andrew didn't give it much thought during their early teenage years. A little more twisting and turning in bed, perhaps, but nothing beyond that. And, as always, he tried very hard to wish the problems away. Not so with his lover who worried about the home situation a great deal, especially since the boys and he were under the same roof.

Time moved quickly as financial demands were not going away and, instead, were getting worse. Credit cards had long since been maxed out and now totaled $25,000. It didn't seem possible that so much money could disappear so quickly. They had nothing to show for it beyond a great deal of self-indulgence. Their apartment was a showcase but now he wished that they could take back some of the money that had been spent making it look so beautiful. His lover was much more attached to the condo and to the whole concept of ownership. For his partner, it was a forever place and any threat of losing it was inconceivable. The days passed by in a blur as the dreadful reality of loss came closer to the surface. Tempers went beyond occasional outbursts and became the norm. It was another one of his partner's continuing liabilities (along with procrastination). So much confusion and frustration and only the replaying of good times kept some sense of order. Andrew wanted in the worst way to not create upset but the time was rapidly approaching when he would have to exert himself and take concrete steps in dealing with the "what ifs". As weeks turned into months, all sense of hope slipped away. His lover had reported that a final real estate commission had fallen apart and nothing else looked remotely possible.

They were in limbo for what seemed like forever. It bothered Andrew almost more than it did his partner. Andrew needed his routines, always needed to feel settled so that he could proceed with his own fixed patterns. It was all part of his control apparatus, something needed to keep his emotions in check. He was not very proud of this but it did maintain his sanity. Discipline was essential as it kept him in line in terms of regulating overindulgence and assorted other bad habits. It also contributed to his staying physically fit—especially now when he was exercising more faithfully. Each year, he found himself becoming more and more that "creature of habit" although he often wished he wasn't so regimented. He tried to to remain upbeat but that attitude was about to be sorely tested. Andrew had mentally told himself that their apartment would be lost to the bank and that nothing could be done about it. How wrong he was! His partner came to the rescue—at least temporarily. He took the initiative to place a call to Andrew's former bank secretary. She had married and moved to the West Coast where she made some successful real estate investments resulting in considerable wealth. Andrew had stayed in touch with her through the years and had followed her continuing successes. At some point in his banking days, Andrew and his secretary had had some fumbling sex. Not very good for Andrew but she had been transported and it was she who would now enter the picture. Andrew was really surprised that his lover would take such a step but his reaching out would prove successful and she had (amazingly) agreed to advancing them $30,000. A loan on the surface but Andrew couldn't imagine a scenario whereby they would ever pay it back. It was not a final solution but it bought a little more time. That time would prove to be very short and soon they were up against it once again. Over the course of their long relationship, those last few years of their N.Y residency would turn out to be the most difficult. Their sex life had also suffered as the mood continued to darken. The poor real estate market showed no signs of movement, with even the most appealing properties having trouble finding buyers. There were arguments back and forth with lover boy now wanting to expand their search to include more aggressive advertising on their part. And once again Andrew showed his tightwad side. He did finally relent and agree to a $20 advertisement expenditure in the New York Times. There was also a meeting of the minds about lowering the asking price which would give them little "wiggle room" for profitability. Still, almost any reasonable sale was surely better than a bank takeover. Thoughts now switched to what might come next.

New York City was not an option and, so, they began to focus on Provincetown, Massachusetts, that gay mecca on the tip of Cape Cod. They had visited on several occasions but had never been there outside of the summer months when tourists abounded. Winter would turn out to be a much different proposition but they never thought about that. Instead, idyllic memories predominated and heading there seemed like the most sensible goal. The location had a great deal of history behind it—particularly in its destination as an art colony. Andrew's partner had once worked there as a waiter and had a thorough understanding of how the town operated For Andrew, there were memories of his being in a constant state of arousal, enhanced by the male beauties who seemed to be everywhere. So many good lookers and everybody dressed down and on the prowl. He had always wanted to return and work the town on his own(still needing to prove himself elsewhere). As always, inner loyalty worked against that but it still very much influenced his thinking about moving there on a permanent basis. As an earlier visitor, he had enjoyed Provincetown on all counts. He found the sea particularly enticing along with the town's old world charm. It was easy enough to get carried away with all the positives while believing that it was a paradise for 12 months of the year. On a prior visit they had actually investigated the real estate market and found it disappointing. Prices were high and were likely to stay that way and go even higher. A poor New York City real estate market bore no resemblance whatsoever to what was happening on Cape Cod.

The New York apartment sale finally happened, forcing them to move on. Now there would be no more squash racquets and no more work as a teaching pro. His squash career was effectively over as no reasonable competition existed outside the big city arena. He hated to give it up but had little choice in the matter. He tried to remain optimistic but was inwardly disheartened and knew that any serious tournament play was not going to happen. There would also be the problem of what came next in terms of income. Provincetown was, after all, a resort town where summer jobs were everywhere. But—by mid-September, the town was largely emptied out and many places closed down until spring. They would be moving there early in the summer but that didn't make employment any easier. Andrew's coordination didn't extend much beyond the racquet in his hand. He couldn't imagine waiting on tables and, in fact, had done it once in his restaurant days. It had proved to be a disaster as impatience led to all kinds of mistakes. He had surely been spoiled by his health club employment. He loved its atmosphere and the teaching and had a hard time imagining more mundane type work. On the other hand, they needed income so compromises would have to be made. At least he no longer had to worry about his kids education. That had been completed and he had satisfied a vow he had made to his mom. Too bad that all those funds could not now be reclaimed as they would have gone a long way towards solving the current financial mess. As usual, Andrew wished that money concerns would just go away, that he could wake up with a" fat" bank account that required only his management efforts. Of course, dear old dad had worked hard for his "nest egg", something that had not been a part of Andrew's history. Now, though, a real change of lifestyle was in the offering. The apartment sale had happened quickly and was followed by a hasty trip to Provincetown to garner some specifics about new living arrangements. While there, they had pinpointed a sweet condo near the beach and a small down payment was made along with a promise by a local real estate agent to help them secure a mortgage. It seemed to be a good start and during this visit, Andrew had also made inquiries about local health clubs. He discovered a large Mid-Cape tennis facility that was attempting to expand it's squash racquets membership. The club was operated by two young brothers who were full of enthusiasm and hired him on the basis of one quick interview. For Andrew, it seemed almost too good to be true (and it was) as he hoped his world of turmoil could settle down with opportunity in the ascendancy.

There were bad omens on the trip north! They had rented one of those U-Haul trucks and also had engaged a group of local movers who followed close behind as they had no idea of the route. Somewhere along the way, the movers got lost. Andrew's lover also had a major crying fit. He had gone out the night before and had come home intoxicated. This only served to add to the depression of leaving the city. Not exactly what was needed in the close confines of the U-Haul truck. Andrew was straining to put a good spin on everything but that had now become much more difficult. It was times like these when Andrew wanted to run away and be left to his own devices. They had gotten a late start from the city so when they finally arrived in Provincetown the sun was setting and the moving truck was nowhere to be seen. Somewhere along the way they had gotten lost. Worse—the real estate agent had not made any arrangement for electricity which made for greater confusion. They were able to rig up some light from the street although it was far from adequate for unpacking purposes. The moving van did show up some two hours later and that only presented more problems as there was little room for all the boxes that had been unloaded. Now it was Andrew's turn to shed some tears as he wondered if they were ever going to get settled. Eventually, they would make some order out of the chaos, no thanks to Andrew who was good for little more then heavy lifting. He had no design sense and no real idea of how to create a livable environment. It was times like these that Andrew grew to appreciate his lover even more.

More bad news arrived early the next day. Their years of high living would come back to haunt them. Their credit history was a shambles and thus there was no reason for any creditor to consider taking them on. Worse, they had few assets and no sure prospects for income. As such, the condo that had been their oasis had become a "no go". The real estate agent who had been so solicitous was now a foe. No credit at all would be forthcoming and there would be no closing on their new love nest. Andrew should have figured that out long before they made the move. All this had happened just as they started to feel at home. Now, alternatives needed to be scoped out. Andrew also needed to establish some sort of a work schedule at the tennis club. Foolish as always, he had rushed into the job situation without getting any of the specifics of his employment contract. Once again he had moved too quickly when he needed more than just a handshake. So—not surprisingly, he was greeted with more bad news when told that his salary would be nebulous although much like New York, he could keep all lesson monies. Not exactly what he had been hoping for. He tried to keep positive through it all but knew that he needed to do a great deal more then accept so much at face value

They did find a home, no thanks to Andrew. Rather, it was his lover who had traded his familiarity with the territory for contact with a local bar owner. No doubt, his lovely blonde physique and way with words played a big part in making him a winner. Whatever the reason, the barkeep took a particular fancy to his lover and had remembered him well. The owners lived in a fancy downtown condo but also owned a nice house just outside of the town center that gave off ocean views. The owners would make the place available to them although at an inflated price as it was summer and everybody wanted a "bigger bang for the buck". They were lucky since most summer rentals had already been negotiated. It was only momentary good news, however, as there was still no clear-cut direction in terms of how they would support themselves. Andrew's optimistic nature was now sorely challenged and problems would soon multiply. At least the temporary home was a good one. It was quite roomy and set back on a slight hill that made for delightful ocean viewing. It was also close enough to the town center so that one could easily walk or bike at a moment's notice. In light of everything else, they were fortunate. They still had some savings from the city sale but not enough to offer any real sense of security. As for work, Andrew had been so unsuccessful with his various vocations that he was stymied as to where to turn next. He remained in his dream world, subconsciously believing in his capabilities while falsely believing that good work situations would find him. Of course, he had found the Cape tennis club on his own, but the job that had seemed so promising, never got off the ground. The two brothers that owned the club had become the "feuding brothers" and all new plans were put on hold. Just a nice way of saying that Andrew's "services" would not be needed. Starting all over again was not appealing but it had to be done.

He got a small "brainstorm", realizing finally that it would be appropriate for him to turn to classroom teaching. He had worked with kids in New York and thought it would be easy to transfer teaching skills from sports to the classroom. A great idea but like so much else, there would be stumbling blocks. In this case, one particular hurdle that would not be open to him. In order to qualify for full-time work he needed a teaching certificate—especially in regards to a public school system which had much more specific requirements. In order to get that certificate, there was a lengthy process to follow and, worse, costs that were prohibitive (at least in terms of their current financial situation). The best that he could hope for was work as a substitute teacher—a position that might possibly become a long term assignment. All schools needed substitutes but it was not rewarding work as it offered no guarantees and left the recipient on call for last-minute replacement work. Also, students looked upon substitutes as expendable and not deserving of respect. For the kids, it was more or less regarded as a day off and a chance not to pay attention. Andrew knew that he was better than that but the bureaucracy made no allowance for non—certified knowledge. And living on Cape Cod meant fewer schools and fewer chances for substitute work. His partner was also having work problems. His table waiting days had long since passed and a late arrival in town meant that most eateries had settled on a full complement of staff. There was a central employment operation which helped in the overall hiring process for job openings but by mid-June nothing very appealing was available. One could always find work in cleaning positions— housekeeping type work that centered mainly on bathroom labor. And in the end, Andrew did take on a housekeeping job. It was a very low-level position and once again Andrew was following his father's dictum about never looking upon any job as being beneath him. It did, however, highlight his continuing fall from the success ladder. One stumble after another and now the future looked even more desperate. Thank God for having a partner who was always willing to take up the slack if it meant keeping them afloat. That effort would finally result in a cashier position in a downtown notions store. Notions was probably a bad word in that the merchandise centered around alcoholic beverages, pornographic films, and magazines geared to a homosexual lifestyle. Not much of an hourly wage but extras were available assuming one was criminally minded. Andrew convinced him that small amounts here and there would go a long way towards getting them through the summer with a modicum of comfort. There was a small "kick" for Andrew in all of this in that he got his first exposure to all those dirty videos. They didn't exactly inspire him but he found them fascinating although no substitute for what he enjoyed with his lover. Indeed, sex with his partner had only become more intense—no doubt helped by the warm air and the male visuals which were everywhere.

Also, maybe the hard times had increased the need for sex as if to assert that one was truly alive. It brought to mind the sexual need that arose after his father's funeral. The present was hardly the same thing and Andrew had no intention of running "amok". Yet, his partner worked at night which left Andrew alone at the height of the cruising hours. There were a couple of times where he had some drinks at home and headed into town. He made some halfhearted attempts at meeting others and usually nothing much happened. Still, there had been a couple of times where he had indulged in "quickies" and then slinked home feeling guilty for what he had done. The sex almost always involved pretty blonde types looking for momentary thrills. Unfortunately, orgasms of any kind were not helping their financial position. They briefly calmed the nerves but what they really needed was to get down to business and make some sort a formal plan regarding the future. They certainly didn't want to continue holding down low-level jobs and pilfering on the side (Andrew was also shoplifting cigarettes at the local Safeway). Lover boy hated the stealing more than Andrew and wanted out as soon as possible. For Andrew, though, it was just one more rationalization and one more necessity for survival. Indeed, survival would become the operative word during their three-year stay in Provincetown. There was little redemption in that save for Andrew being more determined to center his vocational work on teaching. He had came to the realization that, given the chance, he could make a real contribution to the lives of youngsters. His thoughts now raced to the Fall and the start of a new school year.

He was mad at himself! He should have made a firm teaching commitment long ago—as far back as when he graduated from college. A weak streak within him had led to indecisiveness. He often wondered whether the scars of childhood were ever going to fully heal. Too often, the need to keep the peace. Keeping the peace was a family thing that afflicted both his brother and sister. In their case, though, they had a huge advantage in never having to worry about finances. Not so for Andrew whose life remained a continuing struggle to stay afloat. At this juncture, he once again needed to move quickly forward. He did obtain a temporary teaching certificate, thus permitting him to be a substitute. A decent start although not a notable one. In the throes of reflection he could get excited about actually taking charge of a classroom although he would soon fall victim to the temporary nature of his new vocation. He was essentially a grown-up "flunky", struggling to maintain order. He got a few calls, but, as he feared, he was nothing more than a glorified babysitter. In time, frustrations would only increase. Thoughts of relocation swirled within him for he knew success would never happen in their present location. Andrew and his lover might be surrounded by creative forces but creativity for them required funding and this was sorely lacking. Oddly enough, Andrew felt more sorrow for his lover who surely deserved something better then working as a cashier in a glorified pornography emporium. And when his lover wasn't working at his job, he was constantly having to deal with their living arrangements. Because of the seasonal nature of their location, they had never been able to secure a long-term rental agreement. Try as they might, owners were constantly looking to increase rents during the concentrated summer season which started in mid-May and continued right through September. Andrew was older now (although not a great deal wiser)—still willing to party while recognizing a need for greater stability. Maturity had, at least given him a greater recognition of the value of togetherness. Yet, in very short order his relationship would be tested in the extreme as major changes loomed ever closer. They had moved again, this time into a lovely old house that dated back to Revolutionary days. Lover boy had worked his ingratiating magic once again. It would turn out to be their last summer on the Cape and they would go out in style. As if tender margins were not enough, the latest move would make matters much worse. It was a rustic homestead, charmingly simple and quiet. As usual, his companion had made a showplace out of their new location. They would even have a chance to show it off as out of town friends predominated their social life that summer. Andrew imagined that friends looked upon them as successful financiers—something that was very very far from the truth. The summer jobs (back to the motel for Andrew) would cover the rent initially but would not last once the motel shut down in late September. They were soon living in limbo once again, going from one day to the next with absolutely no security in sight. Soon, the owners demands for rental payment became a constant threat(including daily phone calls). This only made for more shame and strong feelings that nothing was going to improve in their current environment. Andrew did get the occasional substitute teaching assignment but they were spotty. Relocation thoughts now advanced from the possible to the necessary. For a while, Andrew kept this to himself since he knew that any move would require some separation from his partner.

There was really only one logical place to relocate. Andrew had two sons in San Francisco. That modestly sized city made sense on all counts. There would certainly be more opportunities and the place was gay friendly having been one of the the centers of the earlier gay movement. Getting there would be a long-haul as it would involve a cross-country drive in an aging station wagon. The station wagon had been one of the last purchases they had made with the proceeds from the sale of the New York apartment. It was a challenge but Andrew knew he could do it—especially since he was "fueled" at the thought of improving their lifestyle. For Andrew, the three years in Provincetown had been wasted time. His partner was more philosophical and had largely appreciated his experiences. Still, they were in a "rut" and Andrew had no intention of more of the same. He had a pathological attitude against waste(particularly of the human variety) and had been ready to move on long before the move was made. Besides, three years in three different houses was bad enough, never mind the lack of steady employment. Andrew felt that his talents were wasted and that bothered him more than anything. There was also a matter of the cultural vacuum that turned the Cape into a cultural wasteland once the summer season was over. There wasn't even any access to foreign films and Andrew thought he might go crazy were it not for the frequent trips to Boston (1 1/2 hours) to recharge his "batteries". Quite a change, indeed, after having so much culture at their doorstep in New York. Moving to Cape Cod might have seemed glamorous at the time but in retrospect it was a mistake on all counts.

Moving would become a major mutual effort. Andrew would be driving solo across the country. They couldn't very well do it together short of sneaking out in the middle of the night while leaving their possessions behind. His sweet partner would have to temporarily fend for himself, giving Andrew considerable concern about the difficulties involved. There would be no easy way out since the owners had created a predicament in trying to extort rent money that was now considerably overdue. The wifely owner was particularly problematic, overseeing her rental nest like a den mother. She had never been an absentee landlord(as promised) but lack of rental payment now meant even greater intrusions. Lover boy was going to have to initiate all of his powers of persuasion to keep the owners at a respectful distance. Making things even more problematic was the need for a rental van. Ultimately, his partner would have to load up under cover of darkness followed by sneaking away to his family house in Quincy. All of this had brought them to a new juncture. Andrew felt that he should have taken action long before and that all the delay was largely the fault of his "disease" of trying to please. This had always trumped practicality. At least Andrew had finally stepped up with some major action aimed at improving their position. This tended to nullify the bad feelings he felt about himself. He was not too thrilled about the separation involved (it would turn out to be much longer than anticipated) but he knew that he needed to get going and that San Francisco looked to be more sustainable.The last week in Provincetown emphasized extra hugs as well as extra orgasms along with the promise of eventual reuniting.

The cross-country drive was uneventful. Then again, there were no thoughts of detours for sightseeing vistas. It was an assignment that needed to be completed as quickly as possible. At the same time, Andrew intended to be cautious and take advantage of rest stops. He needed to stay alert as a great deal of the trip involved long stretches of monotonous miles. There also was one patch of icy, snowy, almost blinding weather as a cold front moved across one of the Great Lakes. It terrified him watching cars and trucks skidding off the turnpike with no exit in sight for miles. However, luck stayed on his side and the rest of the journey was almost relaxing. At least, he would have a roof over his head upon arrival in San Francisco. He was also blessed with a son having the same name. This would give him access to some much needed credit which he intended to use during the course of the salvation process.

He quickly settled into his California location. Then again, speed was of the essence. Establishing his own living quarters was paramount as living with his son was going to be difficult at best. He might love his son but living under the same roof was torture almost beyond contemplation. He wanted "out" as quickly as possible although knew that it might be something of a long process. At the same time, he respected his son and didn't want to upset the boy's routine. His older son had inherited some of Andrew's habits which came with mixed signals. They were both used to being the controlling male and, as such, neither wanted to "kowtow" to the other. It would lead to several clashes that bordered on physical hostility. His son was also much more cautious than Andrew and this would also lead to further clashes. It only served to provide further motivation for Andrew to get going. Yet, he was in another one of those all too frequent quandaries. Teaching was number one on his mind but, again, he couldn't afford the time or the money involved in the pursuit of a California teaching credential. The state was even stricter then Massachusetts and wouldn't so much as except his temporary teaching paperwork. A full certificate in California required a minimum of two years schooling and he needed work much sooner than that. Of course, the private sector did not require credentials although concentrating purely on private schools seriously limited one's options. Another California "wrinkle" was the requirement for all teachers to pass what was known as the California Basic Educational Skills Test (C-Best). This was a four-hour exam that tested the applicant on the understanding of basic English, simple mathematical skills, as well as writing comprehension. It was not particularly challenging for a four year college graduate but it did require a certain amount of "boning up" which included tutorial time with a knowledgeable expert. It did, thankfully, cost little and could be done while searching for other sources of income. He didn't worry much about it, was frankly just glad to be in a new space and moving in new directions. He was also happy about the temperate climate. Their last year in Provincetown had featured a brutal winter with deep freeze temperatures and exorbitant heating bills.

He missed his partner and their togetherness. He also really missed sex. His sex drive was still overactive and was a major distraction despite his increasing age. Sometimes, he wished it would all go away or not be so constantly present. Sex was another area to which he owed a great deal to his lover. After all, they had met in 1982, the same year that the newspapers began reporting about the AIDS disease that would eventually decimate the gay population. Andrew often wondered whether he, too, would have been a victim had it not been for the love of his life. He still had fantasies but had come to acknowledge that they were better left that way for the reality was never quite the same thing. Nonetheless, he knew that under certain conditions he could easily slip again and find momentary pleasures elsewhere. Drinking could still get him going but now he had to be particularly careful since in San Francisco driving was required if one were to head out to socialize. Fortunately, temptations were not what they once were as bars were much less popular. More and more gay people had settled down with healthy partners. Andrew certainly fell into the healthy category and had become more health conscious with age. Racquet activity might now be in the past but it was replaced by a daily jogging routine.

He did eventually venture into the night but it took some time before he got around to it. One of the problems was living under his son's roof—a son who was much more circumspect about home socializing. A real change from Andrew's old New York routine where the apartment (and later the condo) had been a "beehive" of activity. There were times that his children wondered whether their father was ever going to settle down. They were pleased when that moment finally arrived and thus unhappy with anything extracurricular. His oldest son was particularly prudish about that and Andrew had no intention of flaunting an overnight" trick" on him. Besides, Andrew's oldest was in the process of settling down himself. He had always been attracted to Asian girls and, recently, a Filipino lass had captured his heart. In the back of his mind, Andrew thought that maybe his oldest was trying to prove to dad that monogamy was the proper option and made the best sense.

Andrew did have a certain sense of pride and respect for his son's feelings and had no intention of taking advantage of the boy's hospitality. A particular no-no was bringing home a stranger for sex. It didn't alter his sex drive—just that the rules about pickups would have to be reversed. It did make things more difficult since most strangers were dubious about exposing others to their living quarters. There was also the factor of expense as going out to bars quickly adds up and was an expense that he could ill afford. So—despite his ever-growing need for a sexual outlet, he worked extra hard at pushing desires into the background. He also missed his partner. There would never be any substitute for what they shared—both mentally and physically. Still, there was no denying his lingering need and finally the buildup became so strong that he became determined to share his body with another. He supposed that it was that evil Gemini twin coming to the fore and like so many other mistakes, he rationalized away his wrongheadedness. He kept telling himself that it would just be one time and that he was entitled to it in light of the long absence he had had to endure. It was most unlike him to be so calculating but calculating he would have to be since he needed to make some explanation to his son for his absence. He said he would be visiting a friend of a friend and that he wouldn't be late. His son was actually quite happy with it as the boy needed some alone time of his own.

The evening would turn out to be modestly successful in the sense than an orgasm was achieved. Andrew had made a point of dressing for the occasion. He did his best to give himself the "preppy" look and at least he was still slim and had most of his hair (despite thinning in spots). There might be a few wrinkles creeping up on his skin and certainly nobody was going to look upon him as the sweet new boy in town. In short, he was no longer that young "pup" that once turned heads. Eighteen year-olds would be looking elsewhere but maybe there would be some twenty or thirty year-olds looking for older companionship. Strangely, entering bars still made him nervous despite having lived a gay lifestyle for so many years. He still needed alcohol to get him going and eliminate any semblance of shyness that had always been part of his DNA. So—before he turned himself into major "cruise control", he had a light meal and several cocktails. It was all quite new as he had not spent any time in San Francisco bars. Generally, one now had to tread carefully or risk infection which was then still a death sentence. Dating services and the internet had now become much more important and this combined to reduce the bar scene to more of a social gathering place rather than a headquarters for sexual liaisons. There were still physical opportunities if one happened to be in the right place at the right moment but luck now became much more the operative word.

Thoughts swirling through his head as he got ready to head out into the night for a hopeful sexual alliance. At the same time, he worried about drinking too much. Generally speaking, he had been better about it but he still had a tendency to keep doing it once the first drink settled in. He had only to look to his father for the damage done by excess consumption. And one of his children would later die of it. Alcohol had served him well only in the sense of assisting in the meeting of strangers and the sex that had followed. Now, though, middle-age along with the AIDS controversy had made living in the fast lane much more dangerous. Also, now as he made his way to a pub largely inhabited by younger set, he knew that he would have to tread cautiously. His earlier cocktails had already impaired his judgment and might eventually pose problems for his choice of a partner as well as his ability to drive a car. He probably should have turned back as it was early in the evening and there was a long time to go before closing. His son was also probably worrying about where was "dear old dad". In the end, no excuse would stop him as he was caught up in the moment and really didn't care. Not surprisingly, the "fuel" had only increased his sexual "hunger" and nothing was going to interfere with that. The bar was crowded which was both a good and a bad sign. Crowds made for greater choices but usually translated into longer evenings which delayed pairing off. Andrew enjoyed the sociability of it all, helped in large part by the ready availability of alcohol. It had now been more than a year since he had been out on his own and, in that sense, there was something of a new experience about it. As his eyes flickered around the room he could easily see himself with any number of those who were "prancing" about. Unfortunately, the eye contact was largely one-way—not at all like his more youthful days when a flicker of interest on his part made for any number of choices. Andrew was smart enough to recognize that youth would not come running towards him and was inwardly glad that he had made a long-term commitment elsewhere. Never mind—in that moment he was playing the game and had centered on four lovelies that held particular appeal. He was trying very hard not to drink too much although it was not easy as he was basically just standing around doing nothing. As such, it was all too easy to "sip" away. He recognized that nothing might happen but the urge to socialize had increased. He never could understand how a large percentage of bar people spent so much time standing motionless as if expecting everyone else to make the first move.

In the end, it was a long haul and one of limited pleasures. A nice enough individual—someone who had arrived later and was closer to Andrew's age. It was truly anonymous sex in that there was little communication, no phone calls exchanged and a quick release. At least he had found someone and there was some semblance of common ground in that cuddling predominated. He felt a little guilty and almost wished he could take it all back. At least he appreciated the naked physicality although a sense of guilt stayed with him for days. He largely put it out of his mind by stepping up his efforts to make a life for he and his partner in what would be their new home. His impatience about that only increased as the bar scene faded into the background. Indeed, new conquests were no longer a primary interest. Besides, his lover had always given him the greatest thrills and the warmest feelings. This only served to highlight the fact that extracurricular wanderings were little more than abject foolishness. At any rate, he was now more determined than ever to get going and make some headway. Even his son remarked on what seemed to be a newfound sense of energy.

Andrew applied to take the California Basic Education skills test and sent away for test preparation materials. This required extra time, a luxury that was necessary but one that he could ill afford. The phone calls from his partner back East had been increasing. The boy had escaped but just barely. Andrew was glad that he wasn't there as he disdained unpleasantness. He might accept the reality of it all but it made him even more ashamed about the way life had turned on them. Nevertheless, he felt closer to his partner as his respect for him had only increased. Andrew did detect a degree of pressure, a sense of panic in his partner's voice. It was as if he was concerned that Andrew's move to California might serve as an opportunity for a permanent divorce. That was the furthest thing from Andrew's mind as his commitment was "fixed in stone". For this, he gave continuing hearty thanks for his Scots heritage, his love of family and his need for long term companionship.

A teaching position was going to take time and he needed some other work in the interim. As such, he quickly put together a resume that made him look a great deal more proficient than was actually true. It was deceitful but over the years deceit had become second nature to him. He could do it easily and with a straight face. In this particular instance, it was necessary as he was seeking out a hotel/guest house position. For a change, his timing was good as occupancy rates were high and there were numerous openings for qualified applicants. He felt encouraged and his optimistic nature convinced him that it would only be a matter of time before he could make something good happen. Demand was on his side and it was more a matter of weighing options and coming up with a good choice. In the end, he decided to register with an agency that serviced the city's best hotels. The agency would guide him through a labyrinth that was unfamiliar ground to him. He did think that it was probably a good idea to stay with the more established hotels since they would provide him with union protection. The unions we're good in the sense that they provided the best medical coverage along with guaranteed salary increases. Also, they tended to hire at rates that were much better then those of the smaller, nonunion operations. Of course, union workers were separate from the management level and thus did not offer an upwardly mobile career path. Andrew didn't concern himself with that as he was more than ever determined to settle into a teaching career.

He felt good about what was happening. Maybe there was hope after all and he remained confident that the decision to go West had been the right one. For him, the pieces were finally looking as if they might come together. And after some due diligence, he took a job with one of the better downtown hotels where he would have varied duties that included mail clerking and the occasional substituting for the front desk people. It was a decent living wage that he could build on—one that would also allow him to move out from under his son's controlling household. Andrew also came to an even greater appreciation of the weather despite its lack of seasonal changes. That had its good sides as well in that there were few days of extreme heat and no real frigid air. It suited Andrew just fine. He might miss the summer sunbathing but that was a small price to pay for the absence of severe winter weather. And, of course, he was still close to the sea—just a different ocean. The ocean was still firmly rooted in his blood and he couldn't ever imagine being landlocked. The days seemed to fly by and more and more he was missing his lover and needed to restart their life of togetherness. His blonde beauty, though, was even more agitated and the phone calls had been steadily increasing with expressions of greater desperation. Finally,though, Andrew could be more encouraging as he had come up with a temporary solution to their housing problem.

San Francisco was very problematic when it came to living arrangements. There was a misconception of the city as a large enclave with comfortable room for all comers. In truth, the city proper was dense with a very tight rental market. It was a situation that demanded creativity to fill that void in a reasonable manner. So it was that the concept of rental shares came to the fore. Not much fun sharing living space with a stranger but perfectly acceptable as a temporary solution. It would bring he and his lover together without subjecting them to onerous rental payments. One only needed to be careful in the selection process and be willing to tolerate certain idiosyncrasies in others. After living with his son, that would prove to be a relatively easy task. As the days passed, his lover's desperation took on a new intensity. He assured Andrew that once in San Francisco he would be working within a week. That was probably an honest assessment as the economy continued to boom along and retail openings appeared everywhere. Andrew now found himself with images dancing in his head of their combined income. Romance also made an all too brief appearance as he envisioned the two of them comfortably nestled into their own little private space. With this in mind, his lover would now make the move West for their long delayed reunion. And true to his word, the boy found work within a matter of days—a position selling earrings in a shop set amidst the tourist mob scene on Fisherman's Wharf.

They got off to a good start! Andrew had thoroughly investigated the rooming situation and had settled on an older single man of German extraction who owned a comfortable house just outside the city limits. The fact that it was not in the city proper made the rental price much more reasonable while the location was still within easy access to public transportation. It gave them nothing more than a private bedroom but at least the house was large enough so that they could operate with little interference. They would sometimes cross paths in the kitchen with the owner but overall contact was limited. Best of all, his lover's future looked secure with plenty of upwardly mobile potential. His partner had long been a proven commodity when it came to sociability and this would surely translate into success on the sales front. Ever the optimist, Andrew trumpeted that they would soon generate enough income to move on to a higher level of comfort. For Andrew, success was just a matter of time and, hopefully, a very short time at that.

They were on the move in the finite sense of the word—even the sex seemed better although it had always been the most compelling event of their partnered existence. Andrew never could get enough and never before had he had such a feeling of total completion. With others, he always wanted to move on to a new face and a new body. He still wanted to be fully in charge but slowly that was being replaced by a greater need to share. Maybe he was finally growing up although he rather suspected that his aging body also played a part in his lessening need for others. Age had also made him was less capable of dealing with complications— especially after the trauma of their leaving New York City. And now with a new path firmly established, involvement with others would be seriously foolhardy. He was actually enjoying the challenges of their new start and the opportunity to make something of himself after so many wasted years. He was also proud of how the two of them together had worked out of one crisis after another. Instead, now he started looking happily at their growing bank account on a daily basis. There was also soon a new living arrangement for just the two of them. It was a lovely, bright apartment located in an older building, close to downtown and within easy walking distance of good neighborhood shops. Best of all, it was a relative bargain. The building was rent-controlled and they could move in immediately. It was unfurnished and this meant a temporary lack of household comforts as all of their furnishings were still in storage. His lover had done a yeoman's job in packing up but the cost of transportation across the country was prohibitive and they were not yet able to afford the $7000 required to get it all out of storage. They needed some good credit history for that so temporary furnishings would have to suffice. As always, his partner did a lot with very little so that they were soon living in relative comfort. Once again there was some sense of stability and Andrew intended to work very hard at making things right for the blonde beauty who had so long depended on him.

They breathed easy for awhile! A year or so of peace and comfort, the likes of which they hadn't seen for quite some time. They genuinely appreciated the break after all the trauma that had preceded it. As it turned out, it would be close to ten years before the subject of moving would again come into play. The whole prospect of moving terrorized Andrew as there had been too much of it in the past. In time, though, they would outgrow their new apartment and complications would ensue as storage space overflowed. This was not helped by his lover's hoarding tendencies. Drawers would fill up and the dining room became more of a dumping ground rather than an eating facility . . . Yet, they still managed their comforts and pleasures. Andrew was just pleased to be able to stay put and not have to subject himself to the whims of the Cape Cod tourist season. San Francisco might be a far cry from New York City but it was a great improvement over the backwaters of the Cape. The city sported a couple of good museums and some semblance of theater along with easy access to first run, offbeat movies. Even better, it was a foodie paradise along with gay outlets too numerous to describe. Andrew never cared much about living in the midst of a gay ghetto but there was something comforting about having it close at hand. In general, social mingling in America had advanced and a gay lifestyle was much more commonplace and much more accepted as a natural part of the" landscape". There were still many gay complaints and protests but, for Andrew, the progress had been nothing short of amazing. It helped to live in a large city as there were still stories of gay people struggling in smaller, more remote locations. So—problems still existed but they seemed terribly remote to Andrew. He was probably fortunate in that he had always taken his lifestyle for granted and couldn't imagine it ever being threatened. As he mused on all of this, the settling in process was conquered. And with their bank account replenished, he fully intended to make proper use of the various social outlets available to them. Life was not only short but getting shorter and properly controlled pleasures awaited. San Francisco was a compromise but it was a good one.

Andrew almost began to take it all for granted. (never a good idea). Fortunately, in the past, small glitches had been overcome and just when a major event appeared to derail them, rescue would come from unlikely sources. For the moment, though, the good tidings continued. The job at the hotel had progressed to the point where he had come on board as General Cashier. He had to chuckle about that—a little bit of the "chicken in the hen house" routine. Yet, for the most part Andrew would handle his duties in a responsible manner while resisting larcenous temptations that were a constant threat. Basically, he breathed a sigh of relief over his full-time status while still working on his dreams of teaching. He did pass the California Basic Skills test despite having to take it twice as a result of narrowly failing the math portion. It was an achievement of sorts while offering no guarantee of a job. All the while he continued to apply for teaching jobs in the private sector and actually went on several interviews, two of which had come close to offers. (Or so he was told). Frustrating, but at least he was generating a decent income in the interim and his lover was doing even better. Andrew could only marvel at it all since he couldn't imagine himself doing that kind of work. There was even talk of his partner heading up a new operation in Hawaii. This made for some lovely thoughts of romance in a tropical climate with warm breezes serving as a major aphrodisiac. It would never come to pass and that was probably just as well since any move there would not bode well for Andrew's own career. That career was floundering along with the economy. He would all too soon be laid off at the hotel and found only temporary work at a small private school as a summer counselor. This was nothing more then a high end tour guide position but at least there was some tutoring involved along with trips to kid friendly amusement locations. In the midst of that, some good fortune would come to him from an unlikely source.

Six months earlier Andrew had responded to an advertisement from a small private school that had been looking for a history teacher. It had been so long ago that he hadn't remembered responding in the first place. As such, it was quite a surprise when he was called in for an interview. His lover would be on the move as well. He had become tired of the earring work along with the irksome commute. Andrew had encouraged him to put his talents to better use and, accordingly, he had found a position with an upscale art gallery located in the lobby of one of the best hotels in the city. It would prove to be most fortuitous and, between the two of them, would result in further comforts not experienced since they left New York City. Discipline was again pushed aside although they held back on extreme foolishness. However, weekend nights out were reestablished and theater events of interest never resisted. It was probably a good thing that the theater was generally second-rate and often not worth the effort. Were it otherwise, they would almost certainly have overdone it. Yet, bad habits returned all too quickly and they easily took up that old "life was short "syndrome. It would have been nice to imagine themselves as more mature but that was really not the case. At least Andrew continued to be physically active and with increasing age was even more dedicated to physical exercise. His energy level stayed strong and for that he was truly thankful. He had even cut back on alcohol consumption although occasionally went overboard. All his life he had been surrounded by people with one health problem after another. As such, it made him work even harder on maintaining his own physical condition. Death had been ever present—more so then with most of his other acquaintances. His parents died prematurely and there was also the early demise of his wife and a lover along with the substance abuse and death of his youngest son. So much sadness although it had made him more determined than ever to take any advantages while trying to take better care of himself. He knew that there would be disappointments along the way but he accepted that they were only part of the landscape of life. He would try very hard to savor the good moments and emphasize even more a healthy way of life. His good attitude usually worked in his favor although the bad side of his nature would sometimes reassert itself and he would carry on in an unacceptable manner. Fortunately, his lover was always looking out for him so he always managed to get home safe and sound. It made him even more appreciative of what he had. Still, Andrew wished that he wasn't so judgmental. His lover's temper tantrums always sent Andrew into a tizzy and he always beat a hasty retreat. He knew that it wasn't a threat to their relationship but it always "stung" him as it seemed so mean-spirited. On the other hand, Andrew had major faults of his own—faults that would be demonstrated even more as he aged. These included keeping to himself too much while avoiding people and social connections. Crowds were to be avoided at all costs. He fought this constantly but only had limited success despite knowing it was wrong to stay so within himself. At least he frequently got out with his lover, something his father always resisted. Andrew thought about that a lot and gave even greater thanks for his lover's influence. They did have much in common including intelligence and background and all that went a long way towards compensating for the frequent temperamental clashes and personal habit controversies. Those controversies would only increase as family problems would come to the fore. Andrew tried to take care of problems as they arose. His lover, on the other hand, was a procrastinator, always waiting until the last minute to complete needed chores. There would be piles of newspapers everywhere, a large percentage of which Andrew sneaked into the garbage at opportune moments. And then there was always that temper which often came out of nowhere and always had a vicious tone to it. It would lead to silly arguments and stifle sensible reactions. As noted, controversies were usually avoided—something that Andrew had inherited from his mother who tried always to keep the peace and avoid controversy at all cost. Andrew knew that he was being dishonest to himself but it kept his stress level down and he was grateful for that. Of course, he was no bargain himself. He could also be curt when something or someone displeased him, often curling up into a very restrictive cocoon. All this was going on while telling himself that he would never adapt his father's unsightly ways. This played a large part in his need to control which made it easier to avoid his father's bad habits. It did make him more disparaging of others who tended to be more self indulgent. Andrew might be curious by nature but he was never boastful about his own achievements. Over the years, he grew more and more impatient about other personality quirks and largely left social interaction to his partner. This was also good in that he found living within himself more rewarding then anything on the social front. He would be perfectly happy burying himself within a book without having to listen to others sound off on themselves. At least he was busier now. The school interview had turned into a full time job as a High School History teacher. He would also be responsible for the athletic program both inside and outside the school. It was all not as grand as it sounded as the school only had 85 students, many of them from Asian countries. Still, it was teaching and a full time job at that!!

Solitary evenings at home were becoming more the norm! Theater and dining out were still mainstays but were almost always limited to weekends. Lover boy had found a new source of friends in the art world. They tended to be a much better breed and much more social. This translated into more frequent nights away from the homestead. Andrew had no intention of keeping up with them—especially since it didn't mix with his new responsibilities as a full-time teacher. Lessons needed to be prepared and homework and tests corrected. He also needed to give himself a refresher course on history and geography as it had been years since he had paid any attention to it. Most of all, he needed to be fully rested as the job involved a lot of energy along with staying on his feet for most of the day. And it didn't take long for him to learn that his idyllic bubble had been "punctured". Right up until the first day of school he had visions of handsome, pliable, sweet youngsters respectful of him as a teacher. How wrong that would prove to be! His biggest mistake was believing in the importance of making his students his friends. A nice idea, perhaps, but also very wrongheaded in that most of the students saw it as an opportunity to take advantage. And advantage they would take—to the extent that he was never able to properly control his classroom. That continuing need for approval was once again causing problems. He needed the boys to care about him and as such he would resist raising his voice in disapproval. Getting off on the wrong foot would be a disaster since once a pattern emerges it always proves difficult to alter. The headmaster had been no help in any of this as his philosophy was to stay away except in extreme cases. Andrew also had to contend with the later addition of several delinquents who had no business being in the school in the first place. Those students needed a strong hand to keep them in line. A strong hand he was not and, as such, all the students suffered. The net of all this was that he had a very difficult first year. Although secondary, he did appreciate being surrounded by youth which helped fuel his fantasy life. Several of the more sensitive ones seemed to adhere to him as if recognizing a common bond. It did help him get through some difficult days although he never had any intention of initiating anything physical. Besides, sexy daydreaming did little to soften his stress level.

There was a teachers/investor conference at the end of the school year—something Andrew wished he could avoid. He was worried that his one-year stint might be his last. He was depressed and his lack of control had played havoc with his nervous system and his blood pressure. The latter was of particular concern since it ran rampant in his family and had been the obvious cause of his father's early death. Andrew was also mad at himself for allowing his classroom to be in a constant state of disruption. He vowed to change it all if he was given another chance. The headmaster seemed to like him well enough although the man could be scary at times with mood swings that seemed to have little basis in origin. No doubt the swings were related to what was happening on his home front. These would later provide ammunition for an ugly divorce. But, at their meeting, Andrew had not a clue as to what might come out their discussion. It turned out to be fairly mild. Doubts were expressed but they were non threatening and the headmaster gave him a limited vote of confidence. No doubt his Ivy League education along with his squash racquets victories played a big part in his being partially forgiven.

His lover had no such problems! Indeed, quite the opposite, as he was now dealing with a peer group of similar backgrounds—customers of a much higher grade than had existed in the earring business. It had all turned out to be a lovely combination, a win-win scenario that was made to order. And, as if on cue, the economy responded. The upbeat news only served to loosen the purse strings as the gallery sales steadily increased. Andrew liked to think that all this might go on forever although inwardly knew better. Still, he continued to upgrade their entertainment budget, finding it all too easy to slip back into bad habits.

The new school year got off to a dubious start as Andrew continued to waver on the dispensing of discipline. He again directed the blame elsewhere as the headmaster admitted several students who would have been better served in military academies. Worse, Andrew had not been pre-warned so interruptions and disrespect came as something of a surprise. So it was that the few would soon upset the many and compromise his teaching efforts. By the end of the first month his nervous system was again upended and he almost dreaded going to school. It was most frustrating since he genuinely wanted to teach and be a positive influence. He had little choice but to stick it out and show some better strength of character. Yet, he always weakened in the face of problem cases. One particular instance stood out when the angry headmaster arrived unannounced into Andrew's disorganized classroom. It was a humiliating moment that had left him temporarily defeated.

His teaching reversals had made something of a cynic out of him! Life still worked its little tricks on him and his naïveté played a big part in that. He had envisioned life as being more simplistic than it was. He knew that he couldn't continue along the same path at school. Something had to change but he hadn't yet figured that out. On this, escapism played its part. There had to be a school out there where the teachers garnered more respect and where learning was a more realistic goal. It surely wasn't the public sector where outrageous activity was even more pronounced. He kept thinking back to his later boarding school days where politeness was much more the ruling force. He now searched the Internet on a daily basis hoping to find a better fit for his assets. Andrew knew that he had many faults but also was aware of his positives and that a large percentage of his students appreciated his presence. Unfortunately, the headmaster was not given to passing out compliments and this made Andrew's position even more tenuous. He had at least passed muster at another year-end review and gotten the green light for a third go around. This was granted in between scoldings for inappropriate classroom events. It had become much more of a challenge in that students had a wide range of diversions—well beyond the radio of his youth. There was television, the Internet, video games, cell phones—gadgets of every size and variety, never mind the drugs that were readily available. It was as if there was a conspiracy afoot to disturb the normal education process. Fortunately, there was still a core majority who wanted to absorb fundamentals and expand their knowledge. Andrew's optimistic attitude still kept him going and more determined than ever to stay the course. He knew that in many ways he was privileged—more so than most. He had been given all the tools and the brainpower to perform at the highest levels. Still— the flaws were all too apparent and often sent him down a wayward path. It was at those frustrating moments when he once again gave thanks for his steady relationship at home, the intensity of which had only grown over their years of togetherness. Few could claim that, especially those in a homosexual liasson. And Andrew did feel that he had gotten better, gotten more centered and less frivolous. No doubt, age played a factor in all of that as he got more concerned about survival and taking better care. He had a much greater respect for the human body and how it often fought against sometimes terrible odds to survive. It always amazed him, for instance, how some overweight people managed to survive despite the seriously extra poundage they carried on their frame.

Andrew kept going, thankful for being fully employed despite the stress level that was involved. For the time being, his present school was the only option. He would've gladly gone elsewhere though nothing appropriate turned up despite numerous Internet searches. He was also racing the age clock that made moving into a new job even more difficult. Thank God for his lover who continued to record one success after another, adding significant funds to their joint bank account. Nevertheless, he couldn't entirely relax knowing that nasty turns happened when you least expected them. He tried to not be cynical about this, just realistic, since all too often they had been jolted out of their happiness routines. The art business could be fickle and more than anything else, was dependent on a healthy economy. People were buyers only when they were comfortable about their assets. It was a discretionary pleasure, not one of the necessities of life. So—there was always an element of worry surrounding their lifestyle. It was surely a good thing that Andrew was not overly concerned although the same could not be said for his lover who tended to worry about everything. Still, the high life always beckoned and was easy enough as it was well ingrained in both of them. Lifestyle habits made for a problematic mix as the subject of expenses had to be addressed This was often problematic due to his lover's inbred dislike of the subject of money. He hated to talk about it so Andrew found himself constantly skirting around the subject which always needed to be approached in a rational manner. As a result, situations often drifted and Andrew usually (almost always)retreated in the face of heated resistance to talk about it all. There was also the continuing subject of credit cards. Good times had brought a flood of new solicitations and discipline would often be set aside. Quite a change from the old days when Andrew was totally dependent on his son's credit cards.

Good times would indeed again prove to be illusionary! They did have a decent run—the better part of a year which gave them a false sense of security. Unfortunately, the economy did turn sour and, predictably, the art world was the first to feel the pinch. It happened very quickly! Prior to the downturn, his lover had been generating sales of close to $100,000 per month. This was almost staggering when one figured in a commission of 10%. Too bad that economic tailspin had cut that by more than half, necessitating an abrupt change in habits. No matter what, credit cards needed to be paid and those companies didn't care about a lower income tally. The only solace in all of this was that they were both still gainfully employed albeit with lower overall earning power.Yet, discipline would now be a greater challenge since pleasures had become even more ingrained.

Lifestyle changes were once again front and center. Almost overnight necessary payments seemed almost insurmountable. Credit card debt was a twofold riddle—his own personal liability along with those belonging to his son. His son was generally pleasant enough about it but could occasionally" fly off the handle" as it was a reflection of his own credit. It was surely a good thing that the boy idolized" dear old dad" and that his protests were meek in nature. Credit card debt was a frightening concept—especially for Andrew as it brought back times when indebtedness had overwhelmed him and destroyed his credit rating.

He had been younger than and more philosophical. However, any repeat performance under current circumstances would be a bigger nightmare. Thank God that they were blessed with low rent payments and were able to make minimum payments on credit card debt. Still, retrenchment was in order as Andrew thought back to his father and his maxim that" never a borrower or a lender be". His dad would surely be horrified at the present situation and yet here Andrew was again defying his dad on another one of dad's strong beliefs. Then again, back in those earlier days there were no credit cards so those temptations were never there in the first place. None of this offered any consolation to present difficulties and, as such, were really not relevant. In times like these, Andrew found it very difficult to accentuate the positive and to try and forget that he had largely made a mess of his life. Friends still spoke of envy in the way that his life had been so varied. It had indeed featured variety but it also came with the constant battle to stay ahead of the fray while maintaining a semblance of comfort. In other words, people might be envious but as far as he was concerned it had all been nerve-racking in the extreme—even more so for his lover who was a worrier by nature.

Once again they got rescued from an unexpected source—one that was the ultimate example of the axiom that "it is an ill wind that doesn't blow some good". Lover boy had taken a fall down a badly lighted set of stairs. A leg had been broken, steel rods had been inserted and a lengthy hospital stay was required. A lawsuit that followed resulted in a $30,000 settlement. Despite the pain, it was perfect timing and gave them a sense of relief as there was now a security blanket that had long eluded them. It would also signal the start of another upbeat phase in their life together. There was something weird about all of this as if some other power was controlling the good and the bad over them. This was patently ridiculous but it did strengthen them as good news seemed to always arrive at the perfect moment when it seemed as if there was no way out. Fortunately, Andrew was grounded in reality and rightfully allowed that it was all just a matter of "dumb luck". Miracles might make for happy thoughts but rarely ever happened. At least Andrew could once again thank his partner for coming to the rescue, albeit in an uncomfortable way. There would later be several surgeries but for Andrew the hurt seemed a small price to pay for the resulting extra dollars in their joint banking account. In the midst of all this there would be another surprise. Overnight Andrew learned that his former employer from his good old banking days was trying to contact him. That bank of his had been acquired by a large foreign institution who had deemed him entitled to a pension. It had been lying dormant waiting for him for several years. All along Andrew had been led to believe that he had not worked long enough to be vested. The foreign bank, though, had different parameters and money had been accruing since he turned 65. It was almost heart stopping and the $40,000 awaiting him would eliminate any immediate bankruptcy concerns. It would not be enough to cover retirement needs but, then again, Andrew had no intention of leaving his teaching job. Indeed, he would still need to be dependent on good working employment which would require even greater attention to detail. Besides, he had long been convinced that staying fully engaged in the workplace was a plus. Anyway, Andrew very much still enjoyed the involvement while always appreciating the youthful atmosphere.

There was something wonderfully comforting about their newfound financial status. Then again, they were old pros with the "ups" as well as the "downs". Creatures of comfort still ruled their house despite background fears of reversals which always lurked. Yet, it was always easy to throw caution to the wind and live a little. Unfortunately, a new interruption had entered their lives. Lover boy's mom was now living with them and was clearly a difficult addition. Andrew resented it—especially the fact that mom was suffering with late stage dementia which required special caregiving. She was 90 years old and basically incapable of doing anything for herself. In time, it would all but take over their lives despite some substantial renumeration from the state of California. The state paid for in-house elderly support services and mom was also getting VA and Social Security benefits. It all but paid their rent so Andrew" swallowed" and tried to take it all in stride. It did, at least, ease the pain of the loss of income from declining art sales. Realistically, Andrew appreciated what his lover was doing and there really was no choice short of ignoring the woman and putting her under State care. Nevertheless, for Andrew the interruption was close to intolerable—especially when he realized that it was only going to get worse. Routine would no longer become the operating word. Schedules would have to be rearranged to accommodate a third-party who required a great deal of attention. Andrew" boiled" inside trying to make peace with it. Her arrival had been the trigger for them to move to larger quarters. The thought unsettled Andrew after all that shifting about on the Cape. Those events had been so upsetting that he would've been happy to never have moved again. Finally, though, they were getting on each other's nerves to such an extent that something had to be done. They did eventually luck out in finding a rental home that came with a backyard as well as views of the Pacific Ocean and the Golden Gate Bridge. The move itself was nightmarish but then again all moves are unsettling. It would at least give them enough room so that "grandma" would have her own space tucked away from the main part of the house. Even so, Andrew wished she would just go away. Even dealing with her on a minimal basis was a challenge to any comfortable lifestyle. All plans had to be made with her in mind. And as the disease increased its hold, there was a constant worry about leaving her alone. It was naturally much harder for his lover as it was his mother and he was witnessing a once vibrant lady turning into a cipher. The woman had long since become incapable of entertaining herself and it gave Andrew the shivers just being in the same room with her. On the other hand, wishing her away was not a constructive option since she was bringing in some serious money to their already restricted bottom line. Fortunately (or unfortunately depending on one's attitude), mama was in excellent health outside of those deadened brain cells so there was a good chance that she might go on for several additional years. Of course, the mental conditions would continue to deteriorate so the caregiving would become a slowly worsening chore. Andrew sometimes wondered what he did to deserve all this heartache and was just thankful that he was able to go with the difficult flow. Ultimately, the income was the "trump card" and made the acceptance formula that much easier. At least the lady was easy-going and grateful for every effort made in her behalf. She was amazingly even-tempered—quite a contrast to her son who continued to be subject to frequent temper outbursts. The woman was remarkable and not subject to those dreadful stories of Alzheimer's patients wandering off and exhibiting bad behavior. Andrew could only admire her although she did cause minor havoc with their relationship. Even sex had to be programmed around her.

But—income had become even more important as Andrew's situation at school went from bad to worse. He was always praying for predictability but it just wasn't there. And life on the home front was not helping matters. It all made Andrew apoplectic at times—begging even more for that permanent sense of security that had always eluded him. He rather thought it was nothing short of amazing that he kept positive thoughts turning inside. The troubles at school were beginning to threaten his health—his blood pressure remaining at a high level despite medication. His latest year at school had been met with only halfhearted success. The age-old problem of control with the students had once again predominated. At least the foreign students gave him some measure of respect. Too bad they were only a small percentage of his classes. And for the rest, there seemed to be daily battles of one sort or another. Too often the troublemakers would take over and disturb the teaching process for everybody else. Try as he might, he was just too nice and seemingly powerless to change that. He continued to do a lousy job and now really dreaded going off to work every day. Mental exasperation made for physical upset and changes would have to be made. He had largely avoided stress in the past—mostly by rationalization in dreaming of better days ahead. Time, however, was running out and for all he knew, little time remained. At best, his options to move in a new direction were limited. Meanwhile, the aches and pains continued. He had even used the services of an acupuncturist who dutifully applied the requisite wires and vibrations that calmed tense muscles. It always seemed to him to be voodoo medicine but in this instance he had to admit it helped. Still, it was only a stop gap measure and was really not addressing the root of his trouble. He had always placed a high priority on quality of life and that was now not happening. In the past, he had not hesitated to have a hip replacement when quality of life was threatened. Now, he needed a less stressful job, one giving less insult to his already fractured ego. Choices, of course, were limited and getting more so as the age factor increased. Faced with such limitations, the only solution was to back away from full-time duty and stay at the school with part-time responsibilities. This was all well and good on the surface but it would mean a reduction in salary. At least they had something of a security blanket although that was always subject to market fluctuations. Andrew could only hope that his lover would take up the slack with art sales (a dubious assumption in the midst of a slowing economy). The thought of carrying less of a burden at school perked him up even though he knew that he wasn't addressing his flaws and weakness of character. He might constantly be analyzing himself but that did little good as he never did much about it. Like so many other difficulties, he was sure that it was all father related and connected to paternal domination in his youth. It had to help explain why he dealt so poorly with discipline and why his crippled ego was constantly seeking reinforcement. It was as if he needed the whole world to love him. It was not too much of a stretch to say that most of his activities were geared to make himself look and feel better. He supposed that this also explained his choice of serial bed partners who would look up to him with admiration while acknowledging him as the "commander in chief" of the bedroom.

There he was once again with his thoughts wandering off in a million different directions. There was at least good news as the school year came to a close. Of course, he was already on tenuous ground with the headmaster who, for some reason, continued to support him. In the past, he had dismissed other teachers for much less cause. He was, in short, unpredictable, and that was never a good feeling as the end of the year staff meeting approached. None of the teachers enjoyed those sessions as all were only too well aware that the headmaster cared more for his "kingdom" then the rights of his subjects. There never was much humanity displayed and mood changes were almost guaranteed. Mood changes often dominated on the home front as well and were getting more extreme as mama continued to decline. The caregiving business had turned into a terrible nightmare and seemed to be getting worse on a daily basis. There really wasn't much that his lover could do about it except, as the saying goes, take one day at a time and try to put the best spin possible on their disintegrating lifestyle. Sex had become an even greater challenge as anger and upset on the part of his lover tended to nullify any sexual impetus. His partner often accused him of being oversensitive and he was surely right about that. He needed to be stroked and soothed and given some sense of pride—not too much to ask after so many years of their togetherness.

More thoughts as he got himself mentally prepared for the year-end final confrontation with the mercurial headmaster. It would be partially successful although he had little choice but to sit back and take the criticism, most of which was in order. He was an outmatched "boxer" but then again he was in the wrong about so much of his work that some punishment was expected. He pleaded for part-time work and probably spoke out before the headmaster made the offer himself. In time, he would be fortunate in having even the part-time assignments. Difficult times were in the making. The State of California had stumbled financially necessitating increases in public teacher layoffs. Thus, there would be a sizable increase in the available pool for teaching positions. Meanwhile, public school classes increased in size making a good education even more difficult. Parents agonized over that but also hesitated in spending more for a private education. Most stayed the public course but it did open up some tutoring assignments for Andrew. He needed those although they added little to the bottom line. A new full time job was largely out of the question. Teacher positions in history were quickly filled leaving availability solely for math and science teachers. Additionally, he had that "bugaboo" of old age. Realistically, he was at the mercy of his own school and the take it or leave it offer. It turned out to be a good choice as he would be working entirely with foreign students and would also have responsibility for the school sports program. He just hoped that his tired legs would hold up under all the vertical work. Between years of running and an artificial hip, he knew that he would have to be careful. At least he had gotten a clean bill of health from his physician.

As old age continued to advance, there would be more reflections as he constantly found himself looking back and summing up the sad state of affairs that was his job history. His doom had largely been sealed by early mistakes, a side effect of the dishonesty that seemed almost inbred. At least he had salvaged something through his teaching efforts although even there he had been hampered by a lack of discipline which had resulted in a succession of troublesome days. He was often embarrassed about his vocational labors. Reflecting on those sometimes overwhelmed him. His dad had always emphasized good work habits—something that could not be said for Andrew. Routines were a good thing up to a point but had resulted in very few successes. Somewhere along the way his routines had fallen into an attitude of wanting the best for the least amount of output. He had surely paid a terrible price for that. There had been a lot of "sorry" along the way but in the end he managed to make peace with his teaching efforts. This was obviously not a get rich scheme and necessitated a serious financial balancing act. "Debtor's prison" always loomed and, indebtedness would always be a permanent part of their lifestyle. They would never catch up and Andrew clearly became immune to their situation. In a sense, he took a certain amount of false pride in playing one debtor against another. He found it very easy to rationalize and, in the end, concluded that life was for the living and there was nothing to be gained by worrying about what might happen after he was gone.

CHILDREN

ANDREW OFTEN WONDERED HOW HE had managed to have children. With each passing year, his attraction to women receded and he knew after his marriage consummation that he had made a terrible mistake. Still, he had managed to father two sons, one of whom would die prematurely after years of substance abuse. It was a particularly sad event for Andrew as the younger son was the creative, sensitive one of the two. The older one worshiped him but Andrew had much more identified with the soul of the youngest. Young Peter's (he often referred to himself as Pedro) premature death was inconceivable and impossible to rationalize away. Andrew could only meekly give thanks for the 46 years of life that they had been able to share. He knew that he personally had to keep going but losing one son provided more ammunition for further reflections. Once again, he would attach blame to" dear old dad" who constantly pressured him to have children. That pressure got even stronger after graduation from college. For his father, it was Andrew's duty to carry on the family name. A fear of his father's wrath had led Andrew to a heterosexual marriage. He might never have done that had he been more assured of his need for male companionship.He also wasn't helped by his lack of knowledge about gay meeting places and bars that catered to a gay clientele. He would eventually learn about all of this and it would hasten the breakup of his marriage. In the interim, he could only admire his wife who struggled mightily to bring 2 sons into the world. The boys would be a source of great pride for Andrew despite their problems reconciling to a gay household. Andrew never helped on that score as he paraded a steady stream of bed mates into their living space. He made only a halfhearted attempt at discretion and would usually wave" caution to the wind" and wallow in the joys of male sexual pleasures. The boys eventually came to understand that this was more or less a part of the household routine. They might not approve of it, but, then again, they didn't really have much say in the matter. Now that their mother was out of their lives, they desperately needed their father and generally went along with the new lifestyle. Andrew sometimes resented their intrusion in his love life but it became less of a problem as both sons were soon off to boarding school.With the boys away, Andrew became even more addicted to serial sexual adventures, but would eventually grow tired of it realizing that it was a "road" that would only lead to a bad ending. Unfortunately, his determination to settle down would initially prove to be a terrible mistake leading to a disaster almost beyond comprehension.But—that would be a long time coming and for the most part, Andrew made a major effort at being a good father. He might not be a very patient soul but he instinctively knew that the boys would mature and be more sympathetic to his needs. Anyway, he loved his children unconditionally and fully intended to be their anchor—especially in light of their mother's death. If anything, that death made him even more determined to do right by them, to provide them with the best despite growing financial restraints. Private schools and colleges were big items on the expense scoreboard but he vowed to complete on them. Obviously, each boy had very different personality traits. Initially, Andrew had gravitated to the oldest and the boy returned that love in kind. Along with that, his older son had quickly grown to resent his mother while exhibiting little sorrow upon her passing. For the oldest, only Andrew could command any respect and the boy would often "act up" when Andrew was away on business trips. Andrew rather thought that his own childhood experiences would stand him well as he took on fatherhood. A nice idea but one that did not take into consideration the fact that it was a new generation with new "roadblocks". Indeed, what had applied to Andrew was not particularly relevant 25 years later. Also, new diversions had arrived on the scene—the internet, cell phones, and, more worrisome, new stimulants. Alcohol was still a potential problem but now more dangerous drugs were available. Still—Andrew had comfortably dealt with his own set of addictions so, hopefully, the boys would also find their way. Andrew was overly optimistic as he imagined his sons' retaining all his strong points while growing out of the bad. On top of everything else, the boys had nothing approaching a normal household. And while his oldest son might look up to him, he lacked a certain native intelligence. He was never going to be a scholar and, indeed, he continually struggled with maintaining passing grades. It was a contest just to get through high school and college quickly became questionable. In the end, Andrew would admire the boy's determination to get a college degree but he did it in a very circuitous manner.

The youngest was a different matter entirely. Much as Andrew felt a great affinity for his firstborn, he was also drawn to the youngest because of his creativity and overwhelming sensitivity. The boy was also totally nonjudgmental and accepted his dad and his dad's lifestyle. The oldest, by contrast, was an early opponent of homosexuality and would go out of his way to cover that up with his classmates. He had a hard skin—very different from the youngest who was fragile and could easily fall into a tailspin if Andrew used an offending word or made a hasty criticism. Andrew's worst mistake was not taking into account the fact that it was now a new era with all the new temptations that this implied. Now— reflecting on all of this, Andrew wondered how he would have dealt with so many diversionary choices had they been available to him during his own teenage years. Then again, kids always found a way to escape routines no matter what the era. Andrew did have to deal with an alcohol problem but he did nothing with other stimulants. Even marijuana was relatively unknown, largely brought to light by the actor Robert Mitchum. The later arrival of cocaine, heroin, LSD and, eventually, crystal meth would add to the choices. Alcohol had been bad enough and Andrew certainly never felt that he was missing anything while growing up. He was probably lucky in that his addictive nature might have attached itself to almost any outside stimulant. As for marijuana, tobacco was bad enough and he never thought to stray anywhere else. Now, though, it was a new era with more destructive stimulants that had become part of the mainstream. He knew all about them but foolishly thought that drug problems happened in other, more disconnected families. In that sense, it was not really surprising that Andrew was in denial when drugs came to roost on his own doorstep.And marijuana would only be the beginning. His oldest son had always wanted to be "one of the boys" and needed the complicity of his peers to make a statement of independence. He still loved dad but knew early on that he had to be his own person. This would lead to his reaching out to those so-called bad types who showed their superiority by disobeying rules. Andrew had done a little bit of that himself—thinking he was above the fray. Eventually, that had led to all kinds of problems that took years for him to straighten out. Now the oldest was set to mimic some of those problematic actions. Andrew tried to be sympathetic but that sympathy arrived with an undertone of anger and displeasure. His older son's dismissal from his dad's high school alma mater would also disrupt Andrews routine as he would now have to seek out new school alternatives. Not an easy proposition as most schools were hesitant to take on disciplinary cases. Of course, there were schools that specialized in disciplinary misfits (under the cover of being proper boarding schools). Several advisors recommended a school that on the surface seemed to be a good fit. It would turn out to be a big mistake—so bad that his son would run away and disappear into the night much as Andrew had done in an earlier "incarceration". Try as he might to keep communication lines open, Andrew would quickly learn that children will often steer their own way during the growing up process.

The younger son was wiser although even more prone to mind altering influences. His comfort zone was much more tenuous as he had been more wounded from his mother's premature death. Indeed, he had always carried a certain sense of guilt about it despite messages to the contrary. In time, the guilt would be replaced with an overall sense of pain. That pain would only be reinforced by the suicide of Andrew's first lover.—a young man to whom the youngest had developed a major friendly attachment. The older boy had a much harder outer shell but he,too, was subject to fits of depression and other unacceptable behavior. It would all border for a time on difficult living conditions—so complex that Andrew had been advised to seek out a psychiatrist who might supply enough support ammunition to help get both boys on a more productive path. Yet, despite numerous sessions, a more normal path would only be a temporary condition. There would be overall stability for a time but soon enough the youngest would return to his need for outside stimulants. And the oldest would eventually return to his path of non-conformity.

Generally, Andrew's responsibility of having children would become a major burden filled with one disappointment after another. Andrew knew all too well that he bore some guilt for the difficulties although he refused to let that guilt consume him. No matter what, he remained determined to do his best. As an optimist by nature, he eagerly assumed that in time the boys would straighten themselves out and make some good contributions during their adult years. And despite the problems overhanging his sons' futures, he rather enjoyed the challenges inherent in his children's formative years. There were disappointments to be sure but also some moments of genuine "sunlight" which gave him feelings of pride and joy. Andrew did keep his fingers crossed, hoping that the boys' entry into adulthood would ease his anxiety and provide him with a greater cheering section. The oldest would have lots of zigs and zags—at first wanting a communications career. This became somewhat problematic as his limited brainpower denied him entrance into his original choice of a communications school. The youngest had long wanted to be a chef, something ignited during Andrew's restaurant days. At least the boy knew exactly where he wanted to go and that was to be admired. Andrew also continued to take great pride in having a son with such wonderful creative powers—something that had totally eluded him. Nevertheless, it was worrisome as being a chef was akin to being in a pressure cooker— not a good place to be for one who was showing signs of needing outside stimulants to comfort internal devils.

The boys gave off positive signs during their early post college years. Andrew remained alert but was temporarily at peace. The oldest (with help from family connections) gained employment with a California radio station. The work was not much of a mental stretch (fortunately) as it was little more than a simplified public relations position. He did little more than distribute free coupons that were given to the station by assorted advertisers. Andrew thought it a perfect job for him and it would last for the better part of a year. It seemed to be "set in stone" or was until the station was sold and the new owners applied the "new broom" axiom. A whole new slate came on board leaving his son with few other options—at least in the radio field. So it was that the boy went in a new direction, that of a travel agent. He had always been fascinated by the concept of travel and at first it seemed like a positive strategic move. In addition to new vocation efforts, the boy was also moving forward in the romance "department". In this he was no doubt proving to his father that he could maintain a relationship with another—in this case a woman since he had no observable homosexual tendencies(or so it seemed despite the fact that his son had more than normal attachments to male friends). But, as far as women were concerned, his oldest had always been physically attracted to ladies of Asian persuasion. Early on, he had provided a Filipino lady with a green card in exchange for free sex and an arranged marriage. Another marriage would later take place as a result of a trip to Vietnam (travel agent discount!). Both relationships would end in failure despite the formal attachments that had taken place.

The sexual act had always been a problem with the oldest. It totally baffled Andrew as he was at the other end of the spectrum. Yet, his namesake could never sustain a relationship and completing a continuing sexual act had proven to be the principal culprit. Both of this serious relationships had involved intelligent ladies who would find successful careers even as he faltered. At least his son had kept working albeit at low-end jobs. This would become problematic as the economy cratered and he would find himself out of work. His son didn't seem too upset about that and Andrew had begun to conclude that the boy rather enjoyed being unemployed. But—that grim reality still lay in the future. During the course of his two failed marriages and after his travel employment, the boy headed into new career territory. He had always been interested in wine and accepted a job as a salesman with a large wine wholesale operation.

As for the youngest son, he would go in a very different direction. After his graduation from the Culinary Academy in Boston, he would settle in to a series of very good jobs with some highly rated restaurants. After working initially in the Boston area, he would join his brother in California where his so far uninterrupted career path would continue. He seemed to have a knack for establishing himself in first-class eateries, unquestionably related to his considerable talents and his great creative nature. Andrew would quickly become his number one cheerleader for it made him terribly proud about the great success story that was starting to unfold. Those initial glory days would also include his youngster's marriage to a lovely sophisticated young lady. A grand wedding of sorts on a Florida plantation close to the Atlantic Ocean was the setting for the ceremony. Opportunity had opened on all counts although the lurking evil of substance abuse was always in the background. Still, for the time being, the good times continued as the loving couple took an extended honeymoon trip for several months through most of Europe's "hot spots", finally returning to the U.S and visiting Andrew and his partner in the first of their several Cape Cod homes.

Too bad that the good times for the youngest would quickly come undone. Disappointment would be a grave understatement—especially to Andrew who was a disciple of discipline. Then again, he should have realized that what applied to one rarely applied to another. Andrew couldn't understand why the boy couldn't make peace with the guilt he felt about his mother's death. That guilt, combined with the stresses of his occupation, had long given the demons the upper hand. Drink would supply a temporary relief but in the long run, only deepened the hurt. Andrew should have given it more thought although knew that it was common practice in the restaurant business for the workers to gather after their shift for the calming effects of alcohol. Two or three beers(often more) was the usual formula.Having pressure released was understandable except that in some cases it became too habitual, leading to even more serious dependencies. Besides—pressures only returned the next day. Andrew had seen it all firsthand and one of the reasons that he had hired Asian chefs in his restaurant was that they tended to be unflappable. Not so his youngest who took to unfortunate dependencies despite taking up exercise to counter the ill effects of the chemicals. There would be stories of healthy ski excursions and rock climbing as well as yoga. It was as if he was proclaiming to all that he was fit and intending to stay that way.

Andrew let his guard down! The boy's health "kick" seemed genuine enough and Andrew relaxed believing that self-destructive inclinations had been set aside. Wishful thinking as it would turn out to be only a brief reprieve. Of course, there were ominous red flags from early on— even when the boy prepared to march down the aisle, new bride in hand. Even the premature death of the bride's father a few days before the wedding couldn't dampen the overall spirits of such a happy union. Still, the boy had obviously taken to drink early in the day as the march to the officiating minister was very wobbly. At least there would be no problem of consummation on the wedding night. His young son had no problem in that "department". The boy possessed great appeal with his long blonde hair, slim physique and healthy endowment. It was hard to resist, especially when the physical was added to a certain vulnerability that was always close at hand. However, along with the bride and groom, the wedding party itself was a heavy drinking crew. For most of the guests it was a one-day affair but for some it served as a kickoff for several days of "party-party." Indeed, the festivities the next day would get so out of control that a drunk driving ticket would be issued to the newly crowned husband. It would delay their honeymoon trip and his poor wife surely deserved better. For the most part, she was forgiving about it and for the time being decided to join the drinking escapades rather than fighting them. She had fallen in love from the very beginning and wanted him badly-even at the risk of her own alcohol dependency. Much later she would wake up to the damage it was doing to herself and their relationship. Andrew would later learn that heavy drinking had been the rule rather than the exception during their European sojourn. Later,too, during their brief visit in Provincetown, drinking became the central part of the daily activity. Bloody Mary's would be consumed starting at noon followed by "killing time" in the afternoon before the start of the evening cocktail hour. On into the night the drinking would continue. Andrew would rationalize all that, categorizing it as part and parcel of a long-overdue reunion. Later, upon reflection, he would identify it as a new drinking intensity which would only get worse in time. Andrew could only hope that the boy would settle down now that the wedding festivities were played out.

Andrew continued to be much too complacent about his youngest's career and lifestyle.He should have followed events more closely although the truth would have been even more discouraging. Cooking stress had resulted in a case of bad habit excess—staying out late and showing little consideration for his wife. She was having her own dependency problems joining into a common ground of too much alcohol. She had tried on several occasions to express her serious concerns in the direction of the relationship. Everything seemed to center around booze—either at the workplace or in their social life. For the longest time Andrew knew nothing about the major controversy that was taking place. Indeed, it was quite the opposite as he thought that everything was going along quite well and that a happy marriage prevailed. Andrew had even started to dream about a grandchild and at least having one son who settled down in a long-term partnership. This became more imperative as he realized that few good future things were going to happen with the oldest boy. The thought of a child was a happy thought. Andrew and his partner had themselves once given some thought to adopting a child. That idea came and went pretty quickly as they were spending too much time enjoying themselves and not wanting to deal with restrictions. And then, with the arrival of semi-poverty, they couldn't very well afford the expense of a new family addition.

Unfortunately, dreams have a way of shattering. As substance abuse overtook his youngest boy, the marriage would implode and there would be no grandchild. Try as he might, the boy just couldn't get on track and Andrew proved to be of little help to him. There would be good moments—times when outside stimulants were avoided and healthy habits predominated. In the end, though, redemption would be short-lived and a "curve in the road" would result in a precipitous fall. For Andrew, the biggest surprise of all was his thought that his youngest son's career would always trump bad influences. Andrew was always carping on the value of life and the importance of doing one's best in the short time granted to everyone. One would've thought that his young son would have had an even greater impetus to live since he had already survived a near-death experience when barely out of the womb. Difficulties were one thing (everybody has them) but self-destruction was quite another. Andrew knew all about that but had been able to pull back before more serious damage was done. It was beyond Andrew's comprehension that his boy couldn't pull it all together and realize the good that was within easy reach. His addictiveness just wouldn't let go—even to the extent of upending his marriage—one that seemed to have been made made in heaven. He did finally acknowledge his problem but blamed the need for outside stimulants on the stress of his job. To rectify that problem, he switched to daytime employment. He found a job at the local zoo working with the catering department and later took on new responsibilities dealing with lunchtime traffic at a major retailer. The drinking would briefly come to a halt in what would prove to be only a pause in a downward slide. For Andrew, it allowed for some brief breathing space as the boy joined Alcoholics Anonymous and concentrated on health rather than damage. There was even some loose chatter about reunification with his now ex-wife. It would be nice to think that maybe, just maybe he was finally ready to make those positive contributions that should have happened from the very beginning.

Three years of good news passed by very quickly. Andrew gave thanks that his youngest seemed to be taking hold of good health. He was regularly attending AA meetings and was reaching out to those he might have offended in many of his many drunken states. He talked almost excessively of his good vibrations. He seemed to almost sparkle and was proving to be much more diligent about his work ethic while getting high marks from his supervisors. He even arranged for Andrew to take on a summer job at the zoo. Inwardly, Andrew worried about how long sobriety would last but for the time being took great pride in all the positives taking place. The boy was now a lone wolf and sharing living arrangements with his brother. This was a very transient existence with the boys carrying on like teenagers. Not very healthy and potentially a bad atmosphere for trouble (the oldest was still drinking). There were few outside pleasures for either of them beyond reading and movie rentals. This struck Andrew as more "killing time" projects as opposed to ones used to gain new insights. In a sense, his youngest appeared to be in a holding pattern before something else would break loose.

The "break loose" started innocently enough. There was the usual Christmas gathering of the clan. They were a nontraditional family but still one very close knit and almost needy. Andrew's lover always went to great lengths to make it special. This was not an easy achievement as space was limited in their little apartment. Still, a tree was decorated and lights were everywhere (even in the windows). Gifts were piled under the tree, music was in the background and there were smiles galore. Everybody always made an extended effort and spirits were festive. Andrew easily joined in and was overactive to the extent that he went overboard with food and, especially, drink. There was a certain sense of encouragement for all to join in including the toasting of their continued good fortune. Only his youngest felt left out. Realizing that, Andrew made the fatal suggestion of provoking his youngest into joining with a glass of wine. Later, with a clear head, he realized how stupid he had been as no alcoholic was ever satisfied with single glass of wine. Indeed, one glass was the start of what would be many to follow. In the words of AA, it was a slip—repairable only if a mistake was acknowledged and the individual returned to a non drinking state. It was not to be.

The folly of Andrew's action became more apparent with each passing day. His worry "machine" would start anew while a closer monitoring process would begin. Even Andrew was smart enough to realize that this was a no-win situation and one that was totally beyond his control. One never knew from one day to the next what might happen. In this case, any semblance of control would rapidly dissipate. No longer would there be consumption free days. Initially, there were no binges but the daily glass of wine would soon become many more. The switch to a day job was appealing at first but any culinary occupation involves a certain amount of pressure no matter what the hours. In this case, the daytime job only freed up the evening hours, giving the boy plenty of time for after work consumption. Then again, Andrew supposed that drunks will always find time to imbibe. Drunk was a nasty sounding word but there was no getting around the fact that the boy was a drunk. In very short order his sweet nature would become temperamental as he became more disorganized and almost frightening to be around. In the midst of all this, the stock market took a "dive", unemployment soared, people lost their homes, and real estate values tumbled. These disasters would lead to his young son's layoff. Everything seemed to be conspiring to make for more unstable conditions. And the boy had not helped his own cause by arguments, his rationality impaired by alcohol. His performance disintegrated, reflecting a waste of so much talent. Andrew hated waste, particularly in the form of human talent when applied to his own flesh and blood. Having creativity was one thing but it needed to be worked on and demanded attention—attention that was no longer happening. Andrew tried to help-offering positive reinforcement—but it proved to be too little too late. As a father, he had made a terrible mistake and surely should've known better. At the time, he didn't think it through and was playing the role of the consummate family man. As a result, the "floodgates" were now open. His son could now easily rationalize his actions by telling himself that dad had given him the okay. This was reinforced by the instantaneous effect of alcohol on his system after such a long layoff. The pleasure was immediate, much like a beginning smoker who gets dizzy after the first puff. There would now be no tuning back! One drink called for another—something that Andrew could understand all too well as it had also been part of his own history. Fortunately, his love of life had trumped all of his bad habits. And with age, Andrew's discipline had only increased.

A bad scenario would soon become much worse. The bad economy was starting to affect everybody—even those judged to be more valuable in the pecking order. Retail sales dropped precipitously and cutbacks were popping up everywhere. Andrew himself was lucky to still be employed—a condition that would not be passed on to his youngest son. Indeed, the boy would lose a second job—not helped as his temper flared again because of a heavier workload. There was now an even greater need to escape. Andrew continued his effort at making positive suggestions but he was on the sidelines and could do little to influence anything approaching a positive outcome. Much as he had done throughout his life, Andrew triggered a set of internal defenses, preparing himself mentally for any bad outcomes. To date, that always managed to keep him on an even keel-up to and including the death of his first partner. But—that was very different from having to face a bad ending with his own flesh and blood. Some people had referred to Andrew as the "kiss of death" what with the loss of life that sometimes surrounded him. Andrew was now seriously frightened for his son as a loss of work only compounded his drinking crutch.

The boy could have done more! Unemployment might be a growing problem but there were always restaurants hankering for kitchen help. Andrew rightly felt that his son was making little effort to become gainfully employed. Both of his children had been infected by that all too common "disease" of thinking that certain work was below their God-given talents. So it was that the youngest wouldn't consider anything below what he he considered his higher cooking talent. Add to that his alcohol dependency and one had a further formula for rationalization. Credit cards were now being maxed out and any serious discussions became more futile. Eventually, to escape parental judgment, the boy would turn to one of his former employment locations. Eight years ago he had been the head chef of one of the better eateries in Crested Butte, Colorado. It was a French style bistro that, under his tutelage, became a destination. During his earlier stay there, the boy had formed a series of contacts which had given him an "in" of sorts with local restaurant employers. Andrew never liked Crested Butte, looking upon it as largely a hippie retreat and a haven for those inclined to "drop out". Drinking was the default activity, largely because there were few diversions outside of its location as a ski resort. It was all too easy to get caught up in the unhealthy side of the daily routine(particularly in the summer).There was lots of good health to be enjoyed as long as one maintained some sense of discipline. There was good skiing in the winter months as well as major hiking diversions in the summer. His son did practice good discipline during his first stay but that was all in the past and no longer part of the equation. Andrew might be an optimist by nature but there was no avoiding the conclusion that work for his youngest son was now done only to support a drinking habit that had become borderline out-of-control. This was only reinforced through occasional phone conversations (obviously tainted by alcohol). It was only going to get worse. Indeed, the move to crested Butte would prove to be a fatal one. There was something very dishonest about it as he had led his father to believe that he had turned the corner and was going to reestablish his cooking credentials. That turned out to be nothing more than a cover to release himself from his father's prying eyes. Andrew had foolishly taken his pronouncements at face value. Initially, though, the move had at least borne fruit as his son quickly found a job as a line cook at a high-end Japanese restaurant. This was below his skill set but at least it was a cooking job and with a restaurant that had a very good reputation.

Six months later his son would be dead—all the hope and promise gone, the demons finally satisfied. Such a shock—made even worse as certain residents revealed many unacceptable incidences. Sordid details but they needed to be explored so that Andrew could come to some sort of understanding and closure. He learned that his son had worked only sporadically and on several occasions and been sent home after arriving for work in an inebriated state. It was particularly painful to learn that the boy couldn't muster up enough discipline to deal with his job in an acceptable pattern. The coroner had declared the death a case of alcoholic poisoning, complicated, no doubt, by his son's history of difficult breathing patterns, a result of sleep apnea. Whatever the final conclusion, it was all something they could never be properly reconciled. Andrew often thought that he should have been more alert but, really, there was little more he could do as long as the boy was committed to overindulgence. At least his son knew that Andrew was there for him and that gave him some comfort. On the other hand, his youngest had been defeated, no longer wanting to keep going. Andrew could never make peace with that and was particularly surprised at how quickly destruction had taken over. So many questions! Was his son at all ashamed since he had always verbalized that he wanted his dad to be proud of him? On the surface, at least, that seemed to be no longer a part of the equation. One million questions, most of which would never be answered. There really was nothing more that Andrew could do beyond remembering the good times. He would soon find that there would always be the daily reminders of one sort or another to keep his youngest in focus. Over time, his long held parental images would get fuzzier. Not so with his son who had left so early and in such an ugly fashion. The sad fact of it all was that overindulgence of one sort or another had become all too common. Now, it had come to roost in his own household. Many earlier phone calls had gone unanswered and letters religiously written every week would go unopened. It was a clear sign to Andrew that a certain line had been crossed without any thought of returning to more constructive activities.

Despite the sadness of it all, Andrew was not totally surprised. He had readied himself for the worst and the worst it was. There was a service, a very nice, low-key one, largely engineered by Andrew's lover. There had been a cremation—much in line with Andrew's belief that it was the best way to make a final exit. His son's remains were scattered at sea from a shipmaster's tourist boat. A local nondenominational minister talked some pleasing generalities that emphasized the spirit which would always be part of the memory "bank". Andrew was particularly heartened by the presence of his brother and sister who made the long trek from the East Coast. It was a reunion of sorts although certainly very low-key. There was a reception back at the house that was brief as most people were worn out by the sadness of it all. Even Andrew had to excuse himself early. The universal appreciation expressed by so many really helped as a calming agent, soothing the effects of the terrible loss. Memories helped too. There were hundreds of photos of his son's married life to take Andrew back to better times. These were eventually given to his ex-wife who was having an even more difficult time dealing with the tragedy. It added to the sorrow and gave further emphasis to the terrible waste of it all. It also accentuated what might've been. The boy's ex had never gotten over her love for him. In the days ahead there would be constant reminders, keeping his youngest son in the forefront of Andrew's thinking. A continuing sad saga replayed on a steady loop. Of course, Andrew being Andrew,he would keep going, always trying to do his best. At the same time, so many lingering questions kept cropping up. In particular, he constantly wondered if he had done his utmost to promote positive thinking. Perhaps an intervention would have put a halt to the downward slide but doing that had never been part of his thinking—mainly because he had at no point any idea that the drinking had gotten so wildly out of control. He could only hope that the loss was caused more by a history of breathing problems rather than the drunken state itself.

The older boy was a much different proposition but equally disappointing. His two sons might be close pals but they were very, very different personalities. The oldest also liked his drink but did a better job managing it. Initially, Andrew had wanted only one child but the risks of spoiling led to his second son. This was a questionable decision what with a diabetic mother who had been medically advised to cease and desist. Yet, the pregnancy had taken place and a survivor had emerged despite the difficulties involved. There had been all kinds of upsets, including early bleeding and, finally, a long monthly hospital stay and a premature birth where survival became a day to day proposition. Personality quirks quickly developed between the boys and made for challenging work dealing with very different proclivities. In the beginning, Andrew had regarded his oldest as the proverbial "chip off the old block". In many ways that was true save for the intelligence differential. Andrew was also bothered by the way his oldest steadily went out of his way to be an anti-conformist—especially when it translated into his poor choice of friends (which would lead to those numerous disruptions at school). The friends mostly turned into troublemakers and were almost impossible to control—especially by his mother who had no passion or capability for discipline. The boy really needed strong fatherly direction and that was hard to achieve as Andrew was too often away from the homestead for a long periods of time.

Children should be a source of pride and joy but that didn't work out for Andrew. Quite the contrary as they had provided only scattered moments of joy. Even his surviving son had given Andrew little reason to celebrate. His vocational history was a disaster and he had little motivation to work. Indeed, Andrew rather thought that his son would be delighted to never have to work again. Andrew could do little about it and, instead, concentrated on making his own set of contributions. Life for him had now become more valuable and so he largely weaned himself off of artificial stimulants. He felt better without alcohol and relegated the use of spirits to "the back of the line". Exercise had always been a priority but now became even more important as he took up a seriously heavy walking program going up and down hills at a rapid clip. As a result, he felt much better and also was much more conscientious about scheduling doctor visits, be they internal medicine, teeth or skin. Common sense had long since told him that preventive medicine was the key. He just hoped that he could escape for the time being the surprise of a terminal illness. All the while, he recognized that to date he had been terribly lucky to still be standing with so much energy. He intended to do all in his power to keep going.

As memories of his youngest son continued to reverberate, the question marks about his oldest would be front and center. Andrew decided that his oldest would never grow up and settle down as he continued to act like a teenager. The marriage "business" was, of course, a disaster. Worse, the boy seemed to lack any capabilities for self-examination—no doubt in part related to his lack of brainpower. As time passed, sex with another became more remote. He had certainly given up on any form of a serious relationship and would face old age alone. He seemed to be more than happy just hanging out with so called buddies while doing the macho male thing. Most of his male friends came with similar handicaps and no inclinations to make any changes. Andrew knew all too well the advantages of sharing. He might have his own set of problems but the overall value of partnership covered a multitude of sins. Not so with his oldest who had retreated after his disastrous Vietnamese marriage. That commitment certainly could have worked had he acceded to his wife's desire for a family. The girl had settled down quickly, learned English, went to school and got a good job as a medical assistant. In short, she had done her job while missing only a compatible husband who could join with her both physically and emotionally. It had never happened and the storybook wedding would come to a bad end. Andrew couldn't make peace with any of it—especially the part where his son explained that her steady sex drive was turning him off. Having a strong sex drive was certainly understandable as the girl was 22 years old and in love. For her, romance was in the air but it was not being returned in kind. For Andrew, sex had early on been a constant. He was older now and with a diminished drive but even in his late 40s he was having sex three or four times a week. He couldn't ever imagine himself being neglectful about something so important. Of course, there was little he could do about it in terms of his son except to advise and hope that some sort of accommodation would be reached. This largely fell on deaf ears as his son grew to believe that he had made a bad bargain. Once again he had selected a bride who towered over him in terms of intellect and drive while the boy satisfied himself with poor motivation and maintaining the status quo. At least his youngest son had been driven early on by a genuine love of cooking. In his case, however, addiction had trumped creativity and motivation. The oldest might have done a better job in controlling stimulants (although there were later concerns as solitary drinking occasionally made its presence) but he did little to capture any sense of wanting to get ahead or make a difference. All this made for a great sense of overall disappointment which Andrew feared would never change.

He kept thinking back. As the years mounted, the summing up process became an even greater part of his thinking. For obvious reasons, his children would play a large part in that process. Andrew had to admit that over time the boys were little more than an adjunct to his own lifestyle. Still, like most parents he had given his all to his children's early years. Later, he made only a few adjustments to his own lifestyle to accommodate their concerns. There was a certain selfishness to all of this but, at the same time, he expected the boys to carry themselves in a proper fashion and to make something of their so called mature lives. He bore some guilt for their failures but he had worked hard as a single parent despite spending a great deal of time on his own gratification. There had been many mistakes what with the introduction of two lovers and numerous one night stands into the household. The boys had seemingly adjusted to this but based on what happened later, Andrew could only wonder what part this unusual environment played in their maturation process. One might not be able to blame later problems on his oldest's lack of intelligence but what about the lack of motivation? And what of his youngest's chemical addiction? Certainly, at least some of that could be blamed on a family history coupled with a home front atmosphere of carefree consumption. Trauma along the way had unquestionably been a determining factor but there was still a great deal of mystery that would never be fully resolved.

For the oldest, the troubles in his second marriage came to a head in little over a year. He had made an attempt to explain his predicament to his dad. Sadly, the boy's mind was poorly equipped for self-analysis much less philosophy and he did little more than state the facts. The physicality of their married relationship had been discarded, or, as his son explained, he had grown to appreciate their friendship but no longer wanted to be physically involved. This, of course, begs the question of what exactly motivated the boy sexually. A tricky area with no answers forthcoming. The boy just retreated into himself and became what Andrew described as a sexual hermit. It was the final piece of a sad end to hopes for a grandchild. This took nothing away from Andrew's love for his children. It was just a final off putting event to his childbearing hopes. It also turned Andrew in the direction of taking more solace in his own partnership. In this, he could take some satisfaction in recognizing the importance of sharing, both mentally and physically (and with age the mental took a commanding lead). Andrew continued to feel particular sorrow for his oldest boy as he saw in him the fallacy of living the single life. It gave him the shivers imagining the loneliness of it all. Worse, there was nothing he he could do about it.

The marriage would continue to founder as Andrew served as the middleman in a running debate. In this instance, he could all too well understand the wife's frustrations. Not surprisingly, she felt unloved as physical activity waned. It was really only a matter of time before everything would become much more volatile. It continued to be beyond Andrew's comprehension that his son would not make any accommodations—even if it meant Viagra or some other form of stimulation. In short order, his wife refused to accept the status quo. For her, having a child became more and more paramount and this was not going to happen under the present arrangement. Andrew gave her a huge dose of credit and was in total agreement with her feelings. She was basically a good character and had genuine feelings for her husband who refused to make any compromises. Another story with a sad ending. That ending was friendly enough as would be proved by later events. They actually had continuing good communications that included phone and dinner exchanges. And, not surprisingly, the now ex-wife would marry an older gentleman who gave her intimacy and a child. One had to admire the girl's determination to keep moving forward on all fronts. Her English capabilities rapidly increased and, further, she had established herself as a successful medical assistant—all the while supporting a struggling family in Vietnam. She surely had energy and determination and, much to Andrew's embarrassment, had made a mockery of his son's limited talents. There was now little question about the boy having a sustaining relationship. Not surprising, really, as he had a long history of wanting everything his own way. Not exactly a good formula for having a rewarding relationship. Even sex seemed to have permanently disappeared although it was an unapproachable subject for discussion. Just one of the many mysteries that would never come to the surface or be dealt with properly. For Andrew, the boy was missing out on so many of life's pleasures. Worse, the disappointments continued to mount up as his son lost his job and made little effort to find new work. Andrew once again realized that his son would be perfectly happy to forever remain amongst the nonworking. Shameful and, for Andrew, the end of his dream for offspring success.

Endings

Conclusions were hard to come by. For Andrew, there was a certain sadness to it all. His attempts at fatherhood had largely failed and traumas on his own home front had caused all manner of problems with his personal relationships. He felt a sense of panic as time was running out. Signals of those last moments abounded—aches and pains and moments of dizziness combined with unusual elements of fatigue. Almost more importantly, his sex drive went "south" and was made even more difficult with the increasing stress level of his partner. Andrew hated confrontations and needed peace to maintain his own equilibrium. A cause of that had come from his own youthful experience where children were always protected against unseemly action. His own parents had serious disagreements but they were always dealt with behind closed doors. Even health problems were kept out of all conversation loops. Death was the ultimate conversational "no-no". There might be the occasional reflection about a life well spent but that would be the end of it. Andrew was ill-prepared for the assorted difficulties and tragedies that would follow him throughout his adult years. Still, in the midst of all the problems, he had become more determined to push himself forward. He would give dad credit for never despairing or giving up—even if it meant taking on some lower-level employment. And from his mom, the privilege of life itself, the fact that we were all lucky to have arrived. On the bad side, Andrew resented his father for many reasons but his mom came out with a clean slate save for her devotion to dad which limited Andrew's access to her. In most respects, Andrew sincerely wished that he had matured at an earlier point in his youth. It surely would've made it easier dealing with his parents. Of course, life didn't happen that way and there was something to be said for that old familiar quote of everything "in its own time". Still, into the mix came rampant homosexuality which he didn't properly understand until it was too late to avoid serious damage to people who had grown close to him. He had kept his gayness to himself, in large part based on his fear of dad's wrath. There was the additional factor of his father's philosophical rants about his namesake carrying on the family tradition. What was good for dad was also good for Andrew! The real Andrew was a very different human being even though his youthful period was a time when individuality was largely repressed. Children were expected to follow certain paths—particularly amongst those families in the upper classes where youngsters were seen but not heard. As such, it was hard for parents to understand youthful emotions. As he reflected back on all this, Andrew thought it was rather amazing that he got through it all without more serious damage. It would have been much easier had his sexual urges not been thrown into the mix. He was never unhappy about his homosexuality; indeed, he rather enjoyed it despite having problems fitting in. Initially, he thought it was a stage that all boys went through during their growing up years. Yet, even some 60 years after the fact, he would fiercely remember his feelings for Mike that started in the 5th grade. There was something permanently appealing about those golden locks and the fuzzy blond wisps of hair starting to accumulate on his arms. Much like that beautiful boy, Andrew's voice was starting to change and he imagined Mike with the 1st blush of pubic hair and the occasional erection that he was also experiencing.He almost desperately wished that he could see Mike's naked body—the thought of which obsessed him. Adolescents tended to make jokes about private parts but boy private parts were not a joking matter for Andrew. Indeed, he tried not to think about that for it usually gave rise to an erection which could prove very embarrassing . . . He did finally get his wish to see Mike's private parts during an accidental joint visit to the washroom. As anticipated, it was beautiful and would later be the source of Andrew's first masturbatory climax. He only wished that it could've been a mutual action. Yet, instinctively he knew that it was unacceptable and stayed his ground. Still, there was no denying that it had excited him and would eventually lead to his taking a picture of Michael (fully clothed). Andrew's mom had thought it rather peculiar while also concluding that it was a sweet touch. For several years thereafter, Andrew kept the picture inside one of his textbooks. It provided a certain comfort and dreams of something more sustainable. He had no idea what all of this signified. His initial orgasm arrived with a combination of guilt and incredible pleasure. Nobody had discussed any of this with him. Should he be doing this? His body continued to react to outside stimuli so there must've been something okay about it all. His initial feelings centered around Mike but arousal was easily expanded—mostly a reaction from his other male classmates. He kept all of this to himself as friends tended to make fun of all things homosexual and he had no intention of being ridiculed. These sexual thoughts would be but one of several factors driving him into his own private world. There he could exist without fear of any outside intrusions. In a short time, orgasmic guilt became a thing of the past and was substituted by pure pleasure. There was something exhilarating about the fantasy world of naked boys. There would also be a place for girls but they were definitely a second choices. He had moments where he yearned to know whether all of this was okay. Unfortunately, it would be many years before he could locate a trusted partner with whom to direct his questions. He tried to get some answers from "dear old dad" but his father was to be feared—especially as he was heterosexually rooted. This was even true when Andrew reached his mid teens and his father had become even more authoritative. He was remiss in not exploring his feelings with his mom although she was usually otherwise engaged in pleasing his father. For Andrew, it was a lose—lose situation and drove him even further into privacy. There was at least something exciting about this whole new world that had opened up and he looked forward to each day and the fantasies it might bring. Throughout his teenage years, sexual inspirational objects would only expand as he would imagine a longer term male partner.

His timing would later prove to be perfect. As he left his teens and entered the so-called physically productive years, the gay world would open up to him. Once he became alert to it all, serial bed partners became the norm. He kept telling himself that he wanted a long-term relationship but for the time being that took second place to the joys of seeking new blood. He had a knack for others wanting to settle down but for quite some time that would not be for him. His mother's pronouncement that maturity would arrive late seemed to be self-fulfilling. Indeed, a longer-term relationship would not enter the picture until he was well into his forties. Even then he would often resort to fantasy images that had so controlled his boyhood. At least he later had the good sense to realize that a partner would take precedence over continuing nightly exploits. He was lucky in that sense for surely there was something ridiculous about a matchup between a senior citizen and a youngster.

As his body aged, there would be even greater moments of reflection. Now, his brain would have an even greater proclivity for summation, reflecting on past events and plotting as best as he could for the future. Something of an inexact science but he did try to be honest about his feelings and faults and what he needed to do to be a better person in the years remaining. Still, discipline came hard as he could never make peace with his resentment of authority. That resentment usually stayed in the background but could reassert itself at inappropriate moments. His long history of mis-used expense accounts, shoplifting and deceitful tax returns were living proof that his father resentment was still very much a part of him.

Early on, constructive self examination was often overtaken by boy dreaming and the need to reach orgasm. Orgasms for Andrew would take on something of an extended homework assignment. School assignments were quickly completed so that he could get on to more pleasurable duties. Fortunately, he was a good student and, as such, could produce high grades with a minimum of effort. In a perverse way, the sexual portion of his assignments presented greater challenges. With a restricted inspirational field, he would find good visuals far and few between. Nevertheless, the advantages of being in an all boy atmosphere helped in his search. It also absolutely reinforced his homosexual disposition. This would only be heightened by locker room access during sporting events. He might resist a staring posture but glances were all too easy. Andrew was not much of an athlete but all boys were expected to participate in some form of cardio activity. He somewhat resisted this but did look forward to the later access to the shower room. It was at this point in his life that marked the start of his "hit parade" list—a list that would become very important for the next 5 years. His elementary school peers would be the ideal and would provide inspiration for even greater pleasures. He rather enjoyed moving them up and down the list depending on weekly visual moments.

Reflections, always reflections! As a teenager he wondered about others and just how different was he? Maybe all of the sexual business involved different stages of development. Did all teenagers go through a period of male to male attraction? Maybe it was all quite normal but he always sensed that it was a subject not open for discussion. Quite quickly he established a system of eye contact thinking that there might be something to the theory that it "took one to know one". If nothing else, it gave fuel for his fantasies. He soon settled into a routine of masturbating at least 3 times a week, writing down dreams of conquests and holding back on climaxes until the very last moment. This was great fun as it allowed him to express his visual delights in a more concrete fashion. It also made the climaxes bigger and better although it did concern him that his growing obsession was taking up so much of his time. For many months his elementary school blonde desk mate, Michael, stayed at the top of his hit parade list. Michael came with the added attraction of being uncircumcised—something that was relatively rare with most American boys at the time. For Andrew, there was something almost magical about the hidden cock head. He was rather envious of it, believing that it might be the source of even greater pleasure. In addition to Michael, another boyishly handsome blonde new student was added to the top of the hit parade. It made Andrew even more appreciative of his access to the locker room. A continuing bonus of the sporting life! That access would continue even into adulthood as he seriously took up racquet sports. In time, though, that availability would disappear but as a teacher he could still appreciate the nearby images of youth.

Mother was right as his maturity arrived late—much too late for his own good. Thank God that he at least recognized the importance of sharing before it had become too late (as in the case of his oldest son). Thankfully, too, he had inherited from his mom an appreciation for the gifts of life and, with it, a greater understanding of the importance of having a partner. Andrew's youngest son had been defeated by substance abuse and the oldest had given up after two failed marriages. The latter had lived for more than 50 years with little to show for it and no likelihood of making any meaningful contributions. Andrew was convinced that the boy would be perfectly happy not working at all, biding his time until dad "passed" ensuring him the proceeds of a small life insurance policy. His oldest might love him but his priorities were surely messed up. Meanwhile, the youngest was gone and that was surely the worst loss of all.

For Andrew, there was no turning back, no way to correct the many wrongs that continued to ply his memory "bank". His own early history with relationships were decidedly mixed so that he was surely no role model for his children. In truth, he could do little more than guide and make pertinent suggestions. In the end, he found himself doing nothing more than crossing his fingers and hoping for the best. He was careful, though, to make sure that his boys understood that he would try to always be there for them. At the same time, they needed to understand that they had to support themselves without financially leaning on "dear old dad". Of course, the best laid plans often have a way of not working out. The oldest would, for the longest time, depend on his father for living arrangements. So much for hoped for success and the boys finding their own way and making a good life for themselves!! At least his youngest had for a time exhibited some flashes of real genius and upward mobility. Unfortunately, this made the decline even more painful. Straightening out steps were brief, but also illuminating and adding to the sorrow of a tragic ending. In a certain sense it had made the early successes an illusion and further confounded Andrew as he couldn't understand why discipline, couldn't have been utilized to neutralize his youngest son's demons. The waste of creativity made the loss even more painful. On top of that, his namesake would provide Andrew with only a few moments of joy. Beyond some fleeting discipline the oldest would make only small contributions worth cheering about. Later on, Andrew would get even more frightened as drinking became the center of his oldest's social agenda.

Age was galloping along and as his body slowed down, Andrew would work extra hard at maintenance—watching his diet, making sure he got daily doses of exercise while religiously taking all medications. He had surprisingly few complaints—only the occasional ache and pain that even younger people suffered from time to time. Importantly, it didn't interfere with his lifestyle. The bones creaked a bit more and the skin wrinkled but he supposed that it was something to be expected. He was really terribly lucky to still stay so mobile and with such good energy. He probably didn't deserve such good treatment in light of some very bad past excesses. No doubt, his heavy sports activity had saved the day and permitted him to carry on. As he turned 79, he had long since outlived his parents, thanks in no small part to medical advances which had kept his blood pressure in check. He was never one to dwell on death but he couldn't help but contemplate the many questions surrounding his last days. He could only hope that it would be a hasty exit with a minimum of discomfort. He did at least better understand his father's fear of a disabling illness, one that might keep him alive but in a paralyzed state. As such, Andrew would often become fearful of any unusual discomforts as they might signal something worse on the way. At least he was an optimist at heart so negative thinking was never permitted to stay around for very long. He also remembered a doctor who had once told him that it was a foolish idea to transpose another's condition upon his own body. Still—bad things tended to happen with increasing age and, like all humanity, he would not be immune forever. But—there was no point in dwelling on it and it was much better to be constructive while practicing everything in moderation.

Best of all, he had been fully stabilized by his partnership that continued growing more dependent as the years progressed. His yearnings for something new had steadily abated and he had made peace with monogamy. All this, despite the fact that he and his lover often operated on totally different levels. They had truly encapsulated the concept that opposites attract. Andrew did sometimes wonder whether he might have been better suited living with a mirror image. Then again, he was often displeased with some of his own personality traits. He was too often a creature of habit—something that displeased him. At the same time, it gave him peace and he had no intention of altering those arrangements. In addition to his own faults, Andrew felt that his lover also failed his ideal on several counts. This would often result in anger outbursts and seething within him that would last for days. Yet, he also had to concede that his lover had many good points, not least among them his devotion to Andrew. Still, the boy couldn't properly channel stress and it was a character fault that would probably never change. Too bad—as it constantly interfered with their togetherness. For Andrew, keeping the peace was paramount and so he would "nurse his wounds" to keep the relationship on some sort of sound footing. He needed a partnership and was willing to do most anything to keep it together . . . He was glad that his mom had always emphasized the importance of sharing. Not for Andrew the lonely existence of a lonely old age. He might at heart be a loner with his own agenda but that only worked part of the time and he really needed to share when it came to culture and creative outlets. He could never imagine experiencing any of that in isolation. So—like a great deal of life there were compromises that needed to be understood. He had seen others waste away in solitude and considered this a form of self-inflicted punishment without any happy endings. His son was living proof of that as the boy's solitude became more ingrained and fixed and would ultimately spell disaster for the concept of sharing.

Andrew was lucky in that the force of his personality and intelligence allowed him to be in charge and capable of bringing another into his orbit. He never could figure out the source of that power—the ability to always maintain a special hold on others, sometimes with hurtful results. No doubt, it had a great deal to do with his poor choices—latching on to people where instability prevailed. For quite some time he appreciated having his "cake" on the home front while enjoying rich tastes elsewhere. He knew this was wrong but for many years he refused to discipline himself. It was easy enough to rationalize this as he told himself that he was entitled to anything he could get as he had missed so many years because of his late coming out. He was mildly ashamed of the fact that he lusted after younger boys. It was all very foolish and he knew it since youth could never offer him any real emotional return. His sons might refer to him as a pedophile but Andrew instinctively knew that he would never act on such impulses.

He often talked about never taking advantage of others, yet he did just that when it came to his own intimate relationships. He was, after all, taking advantage by using his sexual powers to control partners and boyfriends. He was glad (and probably lucky)that most of his earlier relationships were short-lived. And for a long time, he found himself in a quandary between wanting new blood while knowing that he needed to settle down. At least he was smart enough to realize that the pleasures of the body were only momentary and without long-term fulfillment. Fortunately, he did finally settle down with a partner who was totally devoted and came with a wonderful creative nature. Unfortunately, all this came with a sensitivity that was easily threatened and one that resisted criticism. Worse, it came with a tendency to find fault in others no matter who was to blame. Faults could be overlooked when sex was rampant but were much more threatening as sex declined with age. There were days on end when tantrums were all too frequent and destroyed rational conversation. Andrew would find himself trying to stay above the fray but it made for increasing difficulties on the home front. These only increased with the death of his lover's mom and the resultant disappearance of her monthly income. Stress now became the operative word and that was a very bad word when it came to maintaining any reasonable equilibrium.

The stress was at least partially understandable and a set of circumstances beyond his control. His lover's mom would arrive in a near vegetative state, the middle stages of dementia. A very bad condition and, unlike childhood, a condition that was only going to get worse. One could only hope for a slow deterioration before care taking became an impossible job to handle on the home front. Some years hence another disaster would arrive in the form of a brother with a major substance abuse problem. His saloon wanderings had led to a fall resulting in a paralyzed right side. Overnight, one impossible job had become two so that all semblance of a normal home life disappeared. The fallout from all this was greater instances of temper explosions making for an even more difficult living arrangement. There was some sense of déjà vu in this as his father's increasingly poor health had often resulted in harsh words between mom and dad. The raised voices eventually led to separate bedrooms in order to keep the peace. Such would never be the case with Andrew although he often retreated further into his private world. The retreat would eventually lead to periods of calm that would keep things copacetic for short periods of time. And, basically, Andrew knew he had a good mate and had much in common that they both enjoyed together.

He had made the transition into old age with relative ease. The sex might have diminished but it had been replaced with a more conscious effort of doing right, making contributions, not wanting to sit back and limit himself to a steady diet of pleasures. In this he was once again trying to prove his dad wrong. Dad had sold his business and done little after that beyond his written treatise on palms (the growing kind). Andrew had been surprised at how well it had sold. The contents were largely technical

and should have had limited appeal to the general public. Still, Andrew
gave the "old man" credit for at least doing something beyond drinking
and golf. Yet, there was no getting away from the fact that Andrew had
inherited a certain portion of dad's unwanted traits. This was particularly
true when solemn moods and avoidance of sociability were exhibited. Try
as he might, Andrew had only limited success in changing those patterns.
His lover made it easier by attaching himself to more youthful friends.
Andrew had little in common with them, had been there and done that
and didn't choose to revisit youthful adventures. There was just too much
of an age gap for Andrew to join in with any sense of pleasure. It all worked
out quite well in that it gave his lover an outside source of amusement
while not in any way affecting their togetherness. Time was moving even
faster when sixty quickly became seventy. Aches and pains had been
getting worse especially as they involved Andrew's hip replacement which
would most likely have to be replaced again. Some days, he would find
himself limping around and could only give thanks that it was nothing
more serious. The aging process certainly made him more diligent—
whatever it took to keep going while maintaining a good quality of life.
He was good at that sort of thing. He liked to believe that his diligence
combined with a positive attitude had extended his life. Still, there had
been many difficult moments—especially as they related to his knees, legs
and balance.He might not look his age but 80 was rapidly approaching.
He tried not to think about that(it sounded terribly old!!) but there it was
looming in the background, not too far away and reminding him that even
greater care would be required. He had already experienced one bad fall
that could have easily killed him(or even worse, seriously incapacitated
him). A rainy night and too much alcohol in the system were the culprits.
It scared him and he resolved that there would no longer be any late night
bar "crawls". Anonymous sex still held a certain appeal but was now more
of a disappearing act.

Sex, that constant "devil" might have provided a great deal of pleasure
in the past but it also had come with some dangerous side effects. Too
much alcohol had also made for some poor choices leading to minor
injuries. He wondered about his poor judgement and the occasional bad
choices. It was also adultery since he had made a firm commitment to his
partner. It was inexcusable—especially since the be best orgasms came

when he and his partner were "locked" together physically. But—alcohol always spurred him on as his ego raged forward for new conquests. This was doubly surprising in light of his being "anal" about his daily habits. Sex, obviously, was not part of the daily equation, and was another manifestation of his conflict with dear old dad. That conflict was a continuing curse. He would never get the answer to why his Father was so "one note", so unemotional with him, so unforgiving, such a tyrant. Enter sex which not only gave off good feelings but, more importantly, it served his ego and made him "king" in his little universe. Andrew could now be the "top gun," especially when he made a point (as he did) of choosing weaker partners. He saw the advantages of that long before he had his first sexual encounter. And once the good feelings became a reality, there would be no turning back. Indeed, he only became more addicted to it. In some strange way he was finally besting dad. But there was more and a great deal of it was bad. This business of reigning "El Supremo" in the sex department also carried over into other activities. He quickly came to resent any form of authority and that would quickly become a formula for unacceptable behavior. Andrew was actually fortunate that his lover had never left him. There were many excuses to do just that and, indeed, there had been a few of those "leaving" threats. It did make Andrew think that there was something inherently good within himself—something beyond the bad stuff that made his loyalty questionable. That loyalty would loom ever larger as old age further descended upon him.

Senior citizenship arrived awfully fast and, for Andrew, the most bothersome manifestation of that was the continuing decline of his sex drive. It only reminded him of the days when his cock needed little prodding to become fully errect. It was quite ironic that it would be happening at a time when sex in many forms was available on the internet. Maybe there was a message there!! Not too many years before, sexual images were limited to grainy films rented from video stores. Now, though, there was so much available at the touch of a return button. Everything imaginable!! No doubt, some people spent hours looking at it all satisfying one fantasy or another. Where did all those beauties come from—hundreds, thousands, satisfying all manner of needs. Much as he appreciated the visuals, he couldn't imagine himself caught up in all of it.

No matter a hard or soft cock, time was too precious to waste on frivolous sexual pursuits.

Still, he wished that his errrection was more accessible. Conquests still held some minimal appeal but he couldn't imagine making an approach when his penis could offer no guarantees. At first, the little "blue pill" worked its magic. Even half a dose gave off quick results. Modern science at work!! Another plus for Andrew in dealing with dad. Dad surely would have appreciated some aid since his troublesome heart had resulted in the negation of his sex life. Maybe dad thought he would get more inspired by alcohol but that would soon take over his life and lead to mom arranging for separate sleeping quarters. One could say that his dad had been born too soon but those little "blue pills" were only a small part of the problem. His high blood pressure had sealed his fate and no errectile disfunction pill was going to solve that problem. He was, in short, a heart attack waiting to happen. Fortunately for Andrew, he had found relief in those medications that could be combined to keep his blood pressure under control. They were a life saver since, as one medic noted, he would surely have been dead without them. Andrew recognized their need but was unhappy that they came with rapidly increasing errection problems.

Further disappointments would follow. Eventually, the "blue pills" and other sex "helpers" wouldn't work at all or became more of a "hit or miss" proposition. Several times nothing would happen for hours. Mornings tended to be the best time for sex—a time before having to deal with the interfering blood pressure medications. It was all very weird and often psyched him out as he worried about completing the act. Obviously, staying alive was more important than the sex act so he really couldn't complain about his condition. Still, for somebody so "needy" about sex, it was truly frustrating to "push" it aside and make some sort of peace with his condition. He did intend to make every effort to please his lover who had been so supportive for so many years. Yet, there really wasn't any solution as none of the assorted medications helped. Try as he might, the results were largely negative and were bound to get worse as age became an even greater liability. Since there was no going back, he just "curled up" and pushed it down the "priority ladder". And, like most things in life, there was a good side to his condition. It would at least keep him out of trouble with others. No longer would there be any solicitation attempts as he couldn't imagine his ego dealing with a flaccid penis at the expected moment. Wanting to be a "top gun" in the sexual performance arena was now not an option and that was surely a good thing in terms of his partnership. And there was also the good news that there was no longer a need for utilizing the need for alcohol to get him int a solicitation mood. Alcohol, in general, was also becoming a secondary habit, and that was also a real plus for his health. Booze, obviously didn't help with his increasing physical stability difficulties which had also become more prevalent. No longer could he laugh at those advertisements for emergency phones for falling down seniors. As noted, he had already had one close call resulting in 26 stitches in his scalp. It was actually a wonder that he had no more serious side effects than lingering dizzy spells. Indeed, all through his San Francisco years it was a wonder that he had never had a major accident or a drunken driving arrest. Surely, at this point in his life he was better off staying close to home and his partner whom he had grown to love for his continuing devotion and support. That partner was the "real deal", a one man man with no other agenda beyond sharing the latter stages of life with Andrew.

Old memories!! Each day Andrew would find him thinking back to his lost son as well as to a mother who had always maintained that he would be a late "bloomer". He had thought little of it at the time but now he had to admit that it was all too true. He had finally settled down in the true sense of the word while acknowledging positives beyond that silly drive to always wanting to be the "top gun:" His sguash racquet successes had been beyond his wildest dreams and for several years he had settled into a teaching profession that gave off steady rewards. Maybe all of those positives were partially motivated by "daddy" revenge but so what? It was all to the good and that was what counted. He never really articulated any of this to the outside world although it made total sense to his lover. Then again, he had few friends and those contacts he made through his lover were those younger citizens with different priorities that usually involved living in the moment without giving a damn about senior citizen philosophies. It did tend to drive Andrew further into himself—a personality quirk that had only worsened as age became a more limiting factor. His partner had long been the more social "animal" and as such was always prodding him to do more. It still led to heated words although

Andrew did try(somewhat) to improve on his outings away from himself. It was not easy for him and it was not easy for many other senior citizens who had a hard time keeping up with modern thinking that had arrived with so many electronic advances. The internet and assorted mobile devices had taken control and involved a whole new mindset. Andrew had allowed it all to get away from him and was just fortunate that his partner had stayed much more current. Of course, aging along with his depleted sex life only added to his strengthening dependancy. He now needed his partner for so much. Not just for technical support but, more importantly, for looking after him and staying alert for potential health threats. Respect had replaced sexual worship although the sex was still the best whenever it happened. Youth might still hold physical attraction but his long relationship now held "center stage". Support and more support had clearly helped with Andrew's continuing general impatience as well as his growing physical instability and anger over his aging. He often felt useless while having to be cautious in his every move, afraid of falling and making a fool of himself. And curtailed drinking also meant fewer pleasures. He also worried about problematic work situations—work that had long required comfortable mobility.

He tried very hard to maintain a positive attitude in the midst of all this. He did have a great deal for which he gave daily thanks. Old age was no fun but everybody got old and in much more debilitating ways. Many never found their way out of the 60's or mid 70's. At least Andrew still had a perfectly functioning brain. He could read and write and make good sense. And he did get out and enjoy the arts and a good meal. The kids at school had kept him spirited and "in the loop" and even at the library he worked with a largely youthful group. He didn't rally understand the complexities of "mobile this and mobile that" and had no intention of becoming a part of it all. Nevertheless, he had a general idea of how it all worked and very much appreciated the advances that seemed to be happening on a daily basis. He imagined that some people looked upon him as a relic and in a certain sense he did come from a very distant past. His past was a time that was dominated by radio and,later, TV and the simplicities of family life. People were never going back to those simpler times and that was understandable. Still, there was something sad about modernity that demanded so little of human interaction.

Regrets!—there surely had been plenty of those but he no longer wanted to go back and get angry with himself. Enough! The present was much more important as the time slipped away. He had enjoyed the library work but there had been disappointments there as well. He particularly liked working closely with Kyle who had seemed so available and sexual. In former times, he almost surely would have given in to any sexual arrangement. Obviously, that no longer applied and any closeness that once existed would soon evaporate as Kyle was moved to another branch. And,really, Andrew needed to move on and try to find more income. Their household financial problems were steadily worsening and more income was a real necessity. Andrew would miss the library but was not afraid to move on. The challenge of a new workplace held considerable appeal. It was almost comforting that sex was no longer a factor and now bordered on foolishness. There was something ridiculous about older gentlemen chasing after youth and that concept made it easier for Andrew to "groove" on to his partner, to enjoy the myriad activities that had long been such a vital part of their togetherness. He was only a little bit sorry about still having to deal with his partner's anger issues—especially as they applied to financial instability. Andrew could never understand those anger personality quirks. Where did they come from? Was upbringing a problem or did the blame fall on the genes? Whatever it was, it still had a way of stifling conversations that were often most important. They usually worked through them but they often drove Andrew into his "shell". That was never a good thing but Andrew had reached a stage were it was difficult for him to fight back and where, more than ever, he needed a peaceful atmosphere. He accepted the fact that his lover was under a great deal of pressure. Taking care of his Mom and, later, the even bigger problem of his brother had exacted a terrible toll both mental and financially. Understandable, except that Andrew thought it could all have been handled with a little less stridency, a little more going with the flow. Andrew should have known better since his lover had long been a terrible "worrywort"—just too emotional about everything, even when all was "smooth sailing". It might have made for great sex but now more practical matters were the headliners. The difficult financial situation was an area where his partner was least able to cope and it still made for the occasional difficult home atmosphere. It could be frightening at times and more and more Andrew found himself wishing he was somewhere else. At the same time, he did need to be more comforting, more demonstrative, more hug giving. Thoughts like that also brought him back to "daddy thinking". Was his Father that way as well? It was all such a long time ago although he very clearly remembered his Father never showing any love for him—certainly never hugging or even saying that he loved him.

In spite of the difficulties, there had been some good news. They could finally get married, thus ensuring all Federal benefits once limited to heterosexuals. And, come what may, they were in the survival battle together. For Andrew, he had finally come "full circle". With each passing day a deepening love of his partner more and more predominated as they became a closer functioning team.Problems might be lurking every which way but they would face them as one. They would manage—they always had and Andrew knew that they would find a way out with comforts once again predominating. Slowly and convincingly Andrew had made peace with himself. It had surely been an incredible ride.